NORTHUS SHETLAND CLASSICS

‡

Northus Shetland Classics is a series of reprints of some of the keystones of Shetland's literature. The series has been established under the guiding eye of noted poet and novelist Robert Alan Jamieson, and operates with the assistance of an advisory group of local academics and writers. Each volume has an introduction by an expert. Works in Shetlandic and English, and those which combine the two, will be included. The series is divided into four streams:

Poyims / Poetry

Alting / Non-Fiction

Myndins / Memoir

Yarns / Fiction

TANG

A Shetland Story

‡

Northus Shetland Classics

Yarns

TANG

A Shetland Story

by

J. J. HALDANE BURGESS

‡

introduced by

Brydon Leslie

NORTHUS
SHETLAND
CLASSICS

Tang first published 1898 by Johnson & Greig, Lerwick

Introduction first published in this edition

This edition published 2021 by

Michael Walmer

North House

Melby

Sandness

Shetland, ZE2 9PL

ISBN 978-0-6489204-2-7 paperback

CONTENTS

‡

INTRODUCTION

Tang was first published in 1898. Its author was the oldest son of John Burgess who worked as a tailor at the foot of Burns Lane in Lerwick. It was there that Haldane Burgess was born on the 28th May 1862, though the Burgess family had their roots in Dunrossness. The boy became an exceptional scholar, and published two significant works before leaving Shetland to study at Edinburgh University. The first of these, in 1885, under the pen-name 'Wan o' da Boys', was a booklet entitled *A Nicht in Tammy Scolla's But End.* The following year he embarked on his three-year Master of Arts degree, by which time he had also issued *Shetland Sketches and Poems.*

Life in the Scottish capital was electrifying. Burgess was immersed in a world of new thought and particularly the ruminations of radical thinkers, which he found absorbing. He revelled in the opportunity to expand his mind, but this was not an attitude shared by his religious father who admonished his son, warning him not to embrace man's philosophy over the testimony of God.

During 1887 Burgess began to suffer a gradual, ultimately incurable, blindness. It is ironic that the world around him was receding into darkness at a time when he was becoming increasingly 'enlightened' within himself. Undeterred, he completed his degree orally and returned to Queen's Lane in Lerwick, where he continued writing in earnest, coining poems and stories on a typewriter adapted for the blind.

In 1891 he published *Rasmie's Büddie*, a collection of poems written entirely in the Shetland dialect, which was a roaring success, so much so that a second edition was printed the very next year. Thereafter, no doubt heartened, Burgess wrote three novels. He set the first of these, *The Viking Path* (1894), in Shetland's Norse era, and later continued the historical fiction theme by placing *The Treasure of Don Andres* (1903) during the time of the

Spanish Armada. Published between these two, *Tang* is by comparison contemporary with his own time, and certainly constitutes his best work in prose.

'Tang' is a dialect word for a kind of seaweed. Burgess begins and ends his novel with a depiction of these brown blades swirling to and fro among the rocks by the shore; the hearts of people inescapably entangled in the life of their community. The narrative takes place within the fictitious parish of Norwik. The characters who people the story are likewise abstractions from reality; crofters and fishermen, wives and daughters, teacher, minister and laird, each contributing to the interplay of overlapping relationships. The warmth of the vernacular gives them credibility; we know them intimately: "Hoo is du, boy, an what wy is your folk?" But this is no Kailyard School utopia. Burgess is honest, his portrayal cold and unsentimental. *Tang* brings to light the shadow side of the community: hypocrisy, jealousy, malice and scandal.

However, this is not just a story. For Burgess it was imperative that his work convey a deeper world of meaning and hope, and he engages with contemporary issues of politics and religion through the character of Hakki, the local schoolteacher, who identifiably speaks for him. Burgess was by that time an ardent Socialist and utilised his creative writing to promote his political views. Hakki reminds the laird that for centuries his kind had ground the working class in a "mill of hell". He's assertive, but their conversation has an unexpected air of friendliness, both respectful and didactic.

In contrast to his later works Burgess does not focus attention on a struggle between social classes at an economic level, rather he opts to present a people essentially trapped within the confines of their own community; psychologically they are contending with themselves. Hakki is revealed as somewhat allied with the laird, at least scholastically, and Burgess uses this exchange as a device to promote progressive ideas. As the laird's daughter notes, "Pa reads a great deal," and her father's attraction to the teacher is acknowledged: "for now he had someone worth talking to."

In his collection of proverbs, *Rasmie's Smaa Murr* (1916), Burgess wrote that 'Da kirks, laek da sköls, sood be oonder inspectors.' At the turn of the twentieth century, educational improvement was a prime concern and Burgess clearly felt discouraged by the church's meagre contribution to this endeavour. In *Tang* he describes vividly a minister "grapplin wi texts 'at wis da same as guddiks" (riddles). Likewise, his disdain for what constituted religious observance is obvious:

> Hoo mony o da folk, tink ye, goes dere ta worship? Da most o da lasses goes ta shaa aff dir bits o cloes, da most o da lads ta sit an glower at dem again, an da most o da aald folk becaase it's da custom ta go an dey're frichtend for what dir neeburs wid say if dey didna.

Burgess' main objection, however, was to the church's apparent inability to effect moral or ethical change. In one of his many altercations with Peter Mann, the minister, schoolteacher Hakki addresses the issue of dishonesty: "Its eradication is part of my daily work, a part of work that the old, soul-saving machine of which you are an engineer seems quite unable to accomplish." Burgess maintains that dogmatic ideas are meaningful only to the extent that they are an expression of truth: "You can't dispute the effect that Christianity has had upon society," persisted Mann. "Yes, its morals; not its dogmas," said Hakki smiling. "Aald Erti there, accepts your dogmas; and dispenses with your morals."

Burgess is direct; his contempt for hypocrisy is clear:

> You believe that the Eternal Spirit guts the repentant sinner like a herring, takes his old heart clean out of him and sticks a brand new heart in where the old one was … these people have new hearts; they have been

> washed in the blood of the Lamb; they at stated periods feed upon Him; one really would expect them to do something even brilliant after such a process.

Burgess was raised a Baptist and had at one point applied to enter the ministry. He clearly had spent a lot of time in church meetings, the familiarity of which comes across in his often comic depictions, accurate down to the ubiquitous buzzing fly 'that went regularly to the kirk on Sundays.' Notebooks from his youth contain sermons of a very similar style to those delivered by Peter, the minister. I speculate that Peter is, quite possibly, based on an earlier version of Burgess himself. He portrays Hakki as squint-eyed, and if Peter represents his author's former ways of thinking, Hakki is certainly looking in different directions now: "God's idea is development." The conflict that exists between idealism and reality is embodied in their strained relationship. The minister holds resolutely to his dogmatic beliefs, but flails around drowning in doubt following his mother's passing. Yet the most serious charge against Peter is that he lacks the courage to pursue his potential; he resists life – the flesh and blood girl is sitting in front of him but he's thinking about her photograph. Hakki is less than forgiving:

> …there'll be any amount of psalm-singing, and praying, and howling, and any number of these infernal, illegitimacy-producing revival meetings of yours; but for character or manliness, or a common, everyday sense of honour, God help the fool that hopes to find them in the like of you.

In his employment as the schoolteacher, Hakki is largely responsible for educating the rising generation of Norwik's residents. Peter can perhaps be forgiven his assumption that such duties would necessitate an active investment in their spiritual guidance, by which pupils be seamlessly ushered into the fold of the church, but Peter couldn't be more wrong. When approached with an invitation to assist at the Sunday School, Hakki respectfully declines the opportunity: "You are on quite other lines from me. You tell the youngsters in the Sunday School that Adam fell; if I were to come there to help you, I should have to tell them that he rose."

Knowledge of good and evil provides capacity for moral choice. Hakki is a moral compass within the community, Christ-like, 'bending gradually in spite of opposition the whole district to his will.' In an essay penned shortly after the tragic loss of his sight Burgess wrote that 'A man's religion is not a thing all made in heaven, and then let down, and shoved into him. It is his own conduct in life.' Burgess knew both the pain of loss and the will to endure. Towards the end of *Tang* he makes a gentle allusion to the sacrificial life of Jesus – a climactic moment in the narrative. The novel ends suddenly, culminating in one rushed chapter devoid of detail, as if the plot was of secondary importance and, having achieved this didactic objective, Burgess felt he had discharged his duty.

Tang is a remarkable novel, and Burgess is optimistic. With cutting truth he presents an adverse picture of his Shetland community, and against this reality teaches the ethical requirement to be good, to act properly, and contend with that which is difficult. Such moral fortitude is seen to change lives and potentially alter the dynamics of society. Despite its rather hurried ending, *Tang* is an outstanding example of searing realism and buoyant hope, contending motifs that ensure a firmly deserved place in Shetland's literary canon.

BRYDON LESLIE
Lerwick, December 2020.

Da Sea o Life sings evermair

    Da sam aald, siren sang,

An da haerts o men drive here an dere—

    Laek da broon blades o da Tang.

CHAPTER I

PETER

"High dreams on fire with God."—E. B. BROWNING

IT was a warm Sunday in June. The folk had gathered in the kirk at Norwik. As usual, most of them were women dressed in mourning black. The older men sat with their wives and younger children; but the lads and single men sat by themselves. They had squeezed themselves into two pews upon the north side of the kirk, though there were four or five quite empty pews in front of them. Most of the young women were in the four front pews in the middle of the kirk; but they had not squeezed themselves together like the men. There was a hush; but flies buzzed here and there. The Rev. Peter Mann rose in his pulpit and said,

"Let us begin the public worship of God at this time by singing to His praise the one hundred and forty-sixth Psalm."

There was a flutter of leaves. Mr. Mann read the Psalm right through, then gave the number out again, and the folk stood up.

Three men stood up in the square seat just below the pulpit. They were John Jarmson, the old precentor; Hansi Bolt, the chief elder in the kirk; and Jeems Ertirson, who was a younger elder, strange as that may seem. John Jarmson was bent with rheumatism, and one perhaps can hardly say that he stood up in the same sense as the others, but he stood up as far as he could get, and then he wanted only about thirty-five degrees of being straight. He was, as he used to say himself in the language of one of his many callings, "jöst a mention aff o da plumb." John swung round towards the folk like a derrick, and cleared his throat to raise the tune. He began by making a sound like the cry of a calf, and he stretched it out so that the end of it did for the first note in the tune. It was the lively tune which John was wont to speak of as "Waarweek: 'at begins low an ends wi a skreegh." John held his book close to his breast and kept time with the tune by swinging his body stiffly to and fro from the hips and up. He had a very deep bass voice. It was the upper end of this voice he used to raise the tune. Any other part would have been sure to lower it. As soon as he had got it fairly started John left the air to be looked after by the younger women in the four front pews, while he rolled down into his native element, the bass, in the depths of which he kept on playing solemnly about like an old whale, helped by the younger men in the congested pews, and coming up to blow just at the first of every verse when he saw it was time for him to give the folk the note again. He did not really need to give the folk the note; but he was a proud, old body, and since he knew that he would soon be giving up his place to make room for a younger man, he wished, as he had often said, "ta shaa dem aa 'at Aald John wisna atagedder timmer yet." The singing would at times have seemed harsh to the ear of a fastidious stranger; but even at such times it would not probably have seemed so to the ear of God, for it was hearty and was very clearly meant as real praise. The voices were all strong. In the singing of the women you could hear the echo of the breezes that had blown in from the North Sea in the spring and filled their lungs when they were delving in "da voar rig," with many-coloured handkerchiefs about their heads and gowns and petticoats tucked up to give full freedom to their active legs. In the men's voices you could hear the roar and rumble of the sea, with which it was the lot of most of them to have to do as fishermen or sailors. All through the singing, praiseful as it was and lively as the tune old John had chosen was, there ran an undertone of sadness that seemed in keeping with the mourning black worn by so many of the folk. One voice alone was free of it. It was the voice of the Rev. Peter Mann, who stood up in his pulpit and sang with his people. He was a tall, somewhat pale young man of five-and-twenty, with light brown hair, a high brow, big, dark dreamy eyes at that moment glowing with ardour and hope, a well-formed nose, a small moustache a little lighter in its colour than his hair, and a slightly heavy underjaw. On a first look you would have said he had great force of will; but on a second you saw that the mouth did not bear out the promise of the underjaw, and on a third you felt that you must wait till you knew more about him before settling what you were to think. As he stood and sang, his eyes wandered now and then over the congregation. Sometimes he looked up to the gallery, in the right back pew of which sat Mrs. Mann, an elderly, sweet-faced woman in widow's weeds, whom one could at a glance have known to be the Rev. Peter's mother, and from whom he had very plainly inherited his irresolute mouth; while in the left back pew sat

Mr. Black, the laird, a thin, dark man with a critical cast of countenance, and his wife, a little woman with a dissatisfied face, evidently vain, and dressed in distinctly bad taste. Sometimes the Rev. Peter's eyes wandered over the lower part of the kirk, resting for a moment here and there on family groups, on those young men in the congested pews, on the young women in the front, and so back to the book again. He never, as preachers often do, looked through the kirk windows at the beauty of the summer landscape without. Nature had vanished from his mind. For him there was no summer landscape, no mother, no laird and his wife, no family groups, no young men crammed together, no young women in the front. He was in the Spirit. He saw before him but the fleshly tabernacles of immortal spirits. For him there was neither high nor low, rich nor poor, great nor little, wise nor foolish. He forgot at times the earthly meaning of the words he sang, for they were lost in the great wave of praise that he felt pass across his soul. If one had doubted this, all doubt would have been banished when the singing of the psalm was ended and the preacher came to his first prayer. In it his soul shot upward, on strong wings, towards the throne of God. It seemed as though he would by main force drag his people up from earth and time, on, up to Heaven and Eternity, as if he knew that there was nothing real but the Soul and God. At first his voice was low and thrilling, but it gathered strength and passion till it filled the building and each listener felt that this man was in conflict with some mighty, unseen force. But through the wrestling there rang out at times a shout as of a man who conquers—the warcry of a faith that will not brook defeat. This was a new tone to the congregation, used, as they had been, to the sedate petitions of his predecessor, the Rev. Mr. Wood. To the laird, who still had in his mind a lingering reminiscence of the classical mythology of which he had known something once though chiefly in its prurient parts, this man seemed like a Titan climbing up to storm the crystal battlements of Heaven. To Hakki

Perk, the schoolmaster, who sat in the corner of the front seat in the gallery on the preacher's left, and who had thus a view of his "port wharter," as old John used to say, the Rev. Peter seemed more like Prometheus indomitably bent on stealing fire from heaven with which to inflame the dull, slow hearts of common folk, and kindle in them burning zeal.

The prayer was ended. Then came another psalm, the reading of the Scriptures, and another prayer in which the Queen and all other members of the Royal Family were held up to be blessed along with all official persons, and the institutions of this land including even the army and navy on which, however, he seemed to ask a blessing with some diffidence, praying God to hasten on the time when war shall be no more. After this second prayer a psalm was sung again, and the congregation sat down for the sermon, some of the younger women bobbing up and down a time or two before they settled finally. There was the customary chorus of coughing and clearing of throats. The text was the first verse of the first psalm sung. The preacher read it out and paused. Some of the women slipped a clove into their mouths; an old man in the north-west corner of the kirk put a chew of twist tobacco into his; while here and there the youngsters were supplied with a few sweets that represented the fag-end of balance on goods bartered at the shop the day before. These different ways of getting ready for the sermon were however, not so widely used now in the kirk as they had been in the days of Mr. Wood. Mr. Mann had certainly stirred up the folk to some extent.

"Praise ye the Lord. Praise the Lord, O my soul," he said again, in a voice clear but low.

He began by stating that the whole creation owed one mighty psalm of praise to GOD, the Maker and Upholder of it all—one full, vast harmony of earth and ocean; of raging winter storm and whispering summer breeze; of thundering mountain waterfall and tiny, tinkling rill; of wild waves breaking on the iron rocks and ripples laughing in lone caves in calm; of sun and moon and burning stars of night.

"Why this? and yet, why not?" said Hakki Perk to himself in his corner.

Mr. Mann rose through the kingdoms in which life was found till he reached human life and, finally, the soul of man. It was clear this was his goal. He had gone somewhat hurriedly till now; but he had reached the region where he felt himself at home. He looked out on existence from this height. Nature was something lying far below. Earth had a meaning only as a spot on which to set the Cross of Christ. All former ages had looked onward to that point; all future ages must look back. The lightning of God's wrath had struck that Tree and passed into the earth, leaving the ransomed sinner safe. That flash had rent the veil. Through the rifted clouds of wrath that rolled away, shone in the splendour of eternal Love. The glittering shows of Time grew dim before the first, faint streak of glory such as this. The blackness of all human woe and pain grew bright with golden light. The guilt of sin had vanished utterly for him whose eyes were turned to that Cross. What were the puny storms of earth to him, who, lifted by the hand of God from out the weltering deep, was set on high upon the Rock of Ages?

Hakki Perk sat watching carefully the gestures of the preacher, which were eloquent at every turn.

"He'll probably wake Norwik up a little at the first," he thought. "There'll maybe be a revival when the crops are in; but after that? well, after that, most things will go as they have gone before." It was the first time he had heard the Rev. Peter, who had been ordained about three months before. His aunt, Willa Perk, the wife of Hansi Bolt, had urged him to come to the kirk; but he had smiled and said that he would wait a week or two till Peter Mann was done with knocking all the dust, that he could get, out of the bookboard and had settled down to moderate work. But he saw that this stage had not yet been reached. He felt, moreover, that this man had stirred him more than any other man had done for many years. Now and then he glanced round at the folk, and saw that many of them sat with eager faces, drinking in the preacher's words. One or two old fishermen, however, were asleep. They had had a hard week at the "haf." The weather having been quite calm they had been forced to row in from this deep-sea fishing, sticking to the oar for many hours. But others sat there listening, wide awake, with an earnest look upon their weatherbeaten faces, and shaking their heads gently now and then, a sign that they were fully satisfied with what they heard. Some of the older women shook their heads still more. Willa Perk's was moving all the time. She had a summer bonnet, for she was not in mourning, and close beside a big, red flower upon it hung a pink bud halfway out of a bright sheathing of unearthly, green, and it was never still.

Besides Hakki Perk, there was another person in the kirk, who was hearing the Rev. Peter Mann for the first time. This was Inga Bolt. She was the daughter of Hansi Bolt and his wife, Willa Perk. It is well to mention this, for the folk in Norwik said that Hansi had another and younger daughter, of whom Willa was not the mother. Like their "forebears," the old Norsemen who had a married women's property act more than half a score of centuries ago, the Norwik folk saw that a woman is still herself, sometimes to a very marked extent, even though she has been married to a man, and so, in common with most Shetlanders, they gave every woman her own name without minding whether she was maid or wife. Inga sat with her mother in the pew immediately behind the four filled by the younger women. She had a pretty face with finely formed features and a gentle but keenly intelligent expression. Her eyes were of a deep blue. Her hair, to tell the truth, was really red; but she had trimmed her summer hat with bright red ribbon that strongly drew the eye away from noticing the hair so much. Her neck and bust, visible from the pulpit, between the heads of the two girls in front of her, were full and rounded; but she was not so stout as most of her companions. She sat there with her deep blue eyes intently fixed upon the preacher's face. Her cousin, Hakki Perk, had once or twice observed this through the sermon. Mr. Mann drew to a close, his last words thrilling out upon his people in a strong appeal to them to turn their thoughts away from all things earthly to the one great matter of their souls' salvation. He stopped, and there was a deep hush, except for the buzzing of the flies and the stirring of the one or two old fishermen who had been dozing and who felt that it was now time to awake. After a short pause, Hansi Bolt and Jeems Ertirson rose in the square seat, took two long wooden ladles from behind them, and came out through the kirk to take up the collection. Jeems carried his ladle more reverently than Hansi, for he had not been an elder so long. They began at the outer end of the kirk. Several of the folk still had their eyes fixed on the preacher as he sat there in his pulpit with downcast eyes and head a little forward.

Among these was Inga Bolt. Mr. Mann was lost in thought; but the rattle of the coppers dropping into the two wooden ladles brought him back. This sound invariably suggested to his mind his boyish days in his father's shop in Lerwick on busy Saturday nights, when the rattle of the coppers meant that he must be as sharp as possible in all his movements. He raised his eyes. They met the deep blue eyes of Inga Bolt. He felt as though a soul had suddenly revealed itself to him. Here, at least, was one whose heart was stirred. As his eyes took in the girl's face and bust he all at once became aware that, mingling with this first impression there came a new feeling which he did not rightly understand, for it was unlike any he had had since he was quite a boy.

CHAPTER II

INGA

"Eigi leyna augu, ef ann kona manni."—ICELANDIC PROVERB

INGA blushed as Mr. Mann's dark eyes met hers, but her face was sunbrowned and so the blush did not show very much. For a few seconds she met his look, then she turned suddenly to her mother and began to whisper to her something about the collection, she scarcely knew what herself. Willa nodded decently in answer without taking her eyes off the minister, for she had noticed that his look was towards their pew; but, as her eyes were not so good as they had been, she did not see that he was looking straight at Inga. After a few minutes Inga glanced up again from beneath the broad brim of her hat; but Mr. Mann was finding the closing psalm.

Her father and Jeems Ertirson went back into the square seat carrying their ladles with which they had scooped up the few coppers that the parish, being delicate about pressing money upon Providence, saw fit to offer weekly in the kirk.

A little afterwards Inga stood with her mother and Hakki out before the kirk door in the sunlight. Most of the folk, in twos and threes, were going up the green, daisy-chequered slope to the west, while a few held northward along the hillside. Inga had wanted to go on with the other girls, but her mother had kept her back. Willa thought it only proper that the daughter of an elder should be introduced to the new minister as soon as possible. She had kept back Hakki too, but with more trouble. Mrs. Mann had just turned south along the churchyard wall with Mr. and Mrs. Black, who would leave her at the manse gate.

After a few minutes the vestry door opened, and Mr. Mann came out. Jeems Ertirson and Hansi Bolt were with him. Jeems shook hands with him at once and walked off after old John Jarmson, who, bent now at a more decided angle and with his left hand resting on the back of his blue pilot coat, while his right used vigorously his old oak staff, was halfway up the slope. As Mr. Mann stopped, Willa poked her head forward with the same gesture she would have used if she had had a shawl about it and wished to sort her hair away to each side under it before addressing him. The pink bud on her bonnet nodded violently, and her nose which was rather long became very prominent now from the way her head was held. She had her Bible with her folded handkerchief about it in her hand.

"Good morning, Mrs. Bolt," said the minister quietly. They shook hands. Willa's manner showed that she was not quite at her ease. She felt she had three different parts to play. She was an elder's wife, a country woman, and the mother of the prettiest girl in the parish. For the moment she could not fix upon the proper mixture of sanctity, humility, and pride, which her bearing should possess. But her middle part, that of the country woman, took the upper hand, for she was most accustomed to it. It was known in the parish and beyond it that the Bolts were pretty well to do, but they tried hard to hide this by keeping, to all outward seeming, on a level with their neighbours.

"Dis is Inga, my dochter, sir," said Willa quickly, trying to look obliquely at both of them at once, and apparently excluding Hansi from any credit in the matter, "ye'll mind me spaekin o her, sir. Shö's been awa in Fetlar aside her uncle frae da first o da year, an cam haem jöst da last evenin."

"Shak haands wi da minister, Inga," she added, in a tone that showed how apt she was in moments of excitement to forget that Inga was not still a little girl. Inga, nettled at her mother's tone and flushing slightly, gave Mr. Mann her hand, but did not look at him. At the touch of her warm hand, gloveless and not quite soft, he was conscious of a renewal of that curious feeling he had had in the kirk so short a time before when first their eyes had met. He hoped she would look up, but she did not, and his eyes fell only on the red rim of her hat, round which a fly, possibly one of those that went regularly to the kirk on Sundays, was hurrying as if in doubt about the place. Then he noticed that her mouth and chin were visible in the shade beneath the hat-rim, and he looked at them. Suddenly he felt that mouth and chin were saying to him something he had not expected, something quite different from what he had hoped her eyes would say, had she but raised them. He had hoped to see shining through them the light of a soul awakened, a light the sweeter since it shone out from a pure, young girl's eyes. The other undefined sensation was a mere intrusion, part of the earth that always clings and clogs the soul in aspiration. But he became a little bit confused as he found himself almost unconsciously still taking in the girl's figure. Hakki was the only one that noticed this. Inga wore a black cloth jacket, closely-fitting, and fastened at the neck by a little knot of bright red ribbon and an oval, silver brooch. She would have had a brooch with her name on it if she could have got one, but the makers of such things had likely never heard that there was such a name as Inga, and would have thought it hardly worth their while to make perhaps three "Inga" brooches, if they had. Her dress was red merino, with three frills about the foot. She held her small clasp Bible now with both hands right in front of her, her elbows sticking out. Mr. Mann saw the clear outline of her left breast and side against the sunlit grass.

"I hope you enjoyed yourself in Fetlar," said he, "and that you left your friends there well."

"Yes, sir," said Inga, answering his last words only, "dey wer all well." Her voice was low. She gave a small smile by way of full stop at the end of the sentence. Then Hansi, without waiting for Willa, who was of course, in due time going to introduce Hakki herself, said—

"Dis is a bridder-son o Willa's, sir. He's wir skölmester here."

Mr. Mann half turned and saw a rather tall, sharp-featured young man, with a pair of very keen blue eyes, the left one of which looked as if it would have liked to know what the right one was about, for it was trying, though in a somewhat furtive way, to get a glimpse of it across his nose. On his head he had a hard felt hat, and the little of his closecut hair that showed from under it was red. He had a pretty heavy red moustache, was dressed in a light tweed suit, and carried a walking-stick apparently of Japanese extraction.

The two men shook hands.

"My name is Perk," said Hakki, for Hansi's information had been as usual rather general.

"Yes, I know," said Mr. Mann, "and I have two or three times been on the point of calling at the Schoolhouse; but I have been so busy that I have not yet succeeded. I must come soon now, however. I should like to have a talk with you, for we are both engaged in the same great work, I hope."

"I don't know," returned Perk quietly, with a keen glance at the minister, "Religion and knowledge are not always going the same way." Before Mr. Mann could reply, Hansi, who through long experience of Willa knew that the Perks were fond of arguing, a thing he had never been in his life, broke in cheerily with—

"Dis'll be a göd year, I tink, sir. We're hed a misty Mey an noo we're haein a waarm Jöne an dat brings on da coarn sön, ye ken."

"Yes," said Mr. Mann, "we certainly have great cause to be thankful to God for His goodness to us." Willa gave a large sigh. After a few words more, Mr. Mann shook hands with them all again before going. This time Inga raised her eyes and looked straight into his. There was something in the look that seemed to overleap the only relation in which he as yet had realised that they stood to each other, namely, that of minister and member of his flock. He vaguely felt that the girl, by some subtle power she had, had managed to ignore this purely spiritual relation, but his soul was too much filled at present with its own high aspirations to consider all that this might mean. He turned south along the kirkyard dyke towards the manse, that stood about two hundred yards away. When he reached the garden gate he saw his mother near the porch, bending over a cluster of peonies. As he came up she said to him—

"Mrs. Black tells me that they are expecting their daughter home from the finishing-school in Edinburgh early next month." There was a tone of keen interest in her voice.

"Oh, yes," he said, mechanically, and went in to the house.

Inga and her folk went north along the hillside. Hakki kept with them, for he usually spent the Sunday with the Bolts at Taft, going home with them to dinner after kirk.

The three girls, with whom Inga would have gone before if Willa had not kept her back, were walking slowly on a little way in front of them, but higher up the hill. They were, however, far enough away to let Willa, who was considerably uplifted, pass them without the need of speaking. Inga and Hakki were both busy with their own thoughts. But Hansi, in his cheery fashion, hailed them.

"Weel, lasses, ye're makkin for haem," he called.

"Yea," answered Janny Gair, the tallest of the three.

When the Bolts had passed, Janny turned to the other two, Ann Ertirson and Lowra Sharp, and said—

"Na, bairns, see ye Inga? Dat's a fair new hat 'at shö haes on. A body wid a toucht 'at her head wis red anoff already withoot da laek o yon. O, da pride o dat." Ann Ertirson, a stout, dumpy girl with pale yellow hair, laughed approvingly. She generally thought the same as Janny Gair.

"Lass," said Lowra Sharp, a plump, dark-eyed girl with a pleasant face, "I tink du's turnin blinnd. Yon's no a new hat. Yon's her aald hat trimmed wi a bit o new sylk, an it sets her lovely. An as for pride, even if shö hed ony, I winder wha haes better caase. If du wis only half as weel-laek, du wid be prood dysell."

Janny did not like this, for she certainly considered herself to have some pretension to comeliness; though the pretension was, as often happens, too big for the comeliness. In her own mind in fact she felt that in good looks she was a match for Inga any day. She was a large, able-bodied girl; but her face was much thinner than one would have expected from her bulk. This had given her the idea of being "janteel," as she called it, an idea which she carried out by wearing stays some sizes too small for her, a tight-fitting jacket of which the tightness was more conspicuous than the fit, for it made her look something like a marled ham in front and almost gaped between the buttons, and a dark dress that by its shape suggested a more modern fashion than Janny was herself aware of at the time. This attempt to bisect herself at the waist seemed very startling when one first looked at her substantial figure. One could hardly believe but that the upper part was merely stuck upon the lower and could easily break off. But one became reassured on noticing that this was only relative, that absolutely there was plenty of material left.

"Du aye hed a tongue 'at could clip cloots," retorted she. "Sharp is dy name an sharp is dy natur. I'm mebbe jöst as weel-laek as some 'at tinks a hantle [lot] mair o demsells. I'm aye as janteel aboot da middle as Inga Bolt, at ony rate." This was addressed, over the top of Ann

Ertirson's head, to the back of Lowra's, for Lowra was walking foremost of the three. Janny looked down with satisfaction at the black shadow of her own upper section, that fell somewhat restlessly on the lower and broader portion of Ann Ertirson's back, then she glanced after Inga as if to finish the comparison.

"Du's aboot as muckle laek her as a deuk is laek a lintie," said Lowra, with a laugh.

"O, af coorse," said Janny contemptuously. "Shö'll be settin her kep for da minister nixt mebbe. I tink shö's no free o makkin a beginnin even noo."

"Na lass," said Ann Ertirson, in a tone implying that one really should not go beyond the limits of the likely, even in debate, "it'll shörly be Mary Black 'at'll get him. Wir Jeanie 'at's bidin wi' dem at da Ha wis tellin me da streen 'at dey're lippenin her haem noo in twa or tree weeks time."

"An what's Mary Black better as Inga Bolt?" asked Lowra somewhat hotly. "I'm shör Inga is twise as göd-lookin as her, an if it comes ta siller Hansi Bolt haes a hantle mair money i da bank as Robert Black haes, laird though he be."

"Yea, bit Inga haes nae edication, du sees," said Janny in a tone meant to be fearfully cutting.

"Edication?" echoed Lowra, half turning round; "is no her cousin Hakki been taechin her every winter sinn he cam ta da place? I heard her spaekin Engleis ta da towrists 'at wis in Taft da last simmer, an I can tell you 'at Mary Black wi her Scots tongue wis never able ta dö da laek o it. It wis as beautifil as a piece oot o a book; it wis dat indeed, for ean o da jantlemen axed her whar shö wis learned it. Af coorse shö never spaeks it ta ony o wis." Lowra was the daughter of old Magnus Sharp, the shoemaker, who lived at Hooll, a croft near the top of the hill right west from Taft, and she had a touch of the old man's sarcastic humour.

"O, dir mebbe ean or twa mair i da place 'at could spaek proper if dey wanted," returned

Janny loftily, scorning any closer allusion to herself.

"Yon wis a pooerfil sermon 'at we hed da day," said Ann, anxious to get both of them away from the heating subject. They climbed the hill discussing Mr. Mann's stirring sermon with as much animation as the weather would permit.

All that afternoon and evening Inga was much quieter than usual. There was only one service in the kirk on Sundays, so there was a good deal of slack time after dinner; but the Bolts always let Betty Jeemson, the girl who helped them in the house, go home just after dinner to her folk, who lived at Hooll in the next house to old Magnus Sharp's, and Inga got ready tea and supper. After dinner Hansi and Hakki went up into the yard behind the house and sat there on the grass and smoked. When they were gone, Inga turned to Willa and said pretty sharply,

"It's a queer thing, midder, 'at ye can never manage ta mind 'at I'm no a bairn nu. If ye canna spaek wi sense, it wid be better for you ta hadd your tongue."

"My bairn," said Willa, looking up over her spectacles from a volume of the "Christian Treasury" which she studied with great apparent interest every Sunday, "what am I döne?" Inga was taking the dishes off the table and Willa saw by the way she handled them that she was in a temper.

"Döne?" she echoed, "'Shak haands wi da minister, Inga'; da sam as I wis a infant!" Willa understood. On a week day she would have flared up at once and used her tongue, which from constant practice was always in good working order, smartly on the subject of a mother's rights, especially those of such a mother as herself; but on Sundays she maintained invariably a subdued and sanctified manner, and so she merely said,

"So, so, my jewel, I sall notice anidder time." Then she went on with her reading, muttering the bigger words half-aloud, first in syllables, for she was past the stage of taking them only in letters, then in larger bits, and finally, in a satisfied tone, as a whole; occasionally, however, putting the accent on a quite new place which she selected by some inscrutable means of her own and which, at times, gave a reckless and jaunty air to words that had previously borne a very sober character. Inga, with a flushed face, carried the dishes into the kitchen and began noisily to wash them up, a thing unusual in Taft on Sundays; but Willa said nothing. After tea she did the same. In the evening Hansi fetched up their two cows, Flekka and Sholma, from the grassy slope below the house, where they had been tethered, and Inga took the milkpail and went out to them. She set down the pail, turned up her dress and pinned it behind her, leaving her white petticoat to run the risk of being soiled. She milked Flekka first. When she came to Sholma, she apparently forgot to treat that solemn animal with enough respect, for it suddenly lifted its foot and kicked the pail over, spilling more than half the milk. Hansi made no remark. When she was done, he led the cows into the byre and fastened them.

After supper, Inga rose first from the table and went and stood outside the front door, looking at the "voe." That arm of the restless North Sea was lying calm, with the magic light of a Shetland midsummer night upon its waters and over the brown hills that formed its farther shore. The only thing that could be seen upon the glassy water was the big, black flitboat that lay anchored off a short way from the banks with its black shadow showing like another flitboat bottom-up below it. All was so still that the slight noises in the house behind her seemed very loud. Hansi rising from the table to seat himself beside the fire made quite an uproar in the quiet. After a little Hakki came out and stood beside her. He usually teased Inga a good deal when they were together, but this day he had somehow let it be till now. He slipped his left arm about her waist.

"What's du thinking about, Inga? Bob Ertirson, eh?" he asked, in a for him slightly constrained tone.

"Ach!" she exclaimed impatiently, and, turning quickly into the house, went straight up to her own small room under the roof. A few minutes later Hakki was walking slowly away from Taft towards the Schoolhouse which lay to the south-west on the shoulder of the hill. Once or twice he turned and looked up to her little window in the south gable of the house. It was down from the top and she sat by it looking out. It was too low for one to see straight out through, standing up inside the room; but Inga often sat at it on a little, shortlegged, teakwood chair Bob Ertirson had made her, or lay with her knees on the narrow sill quite near the floor and her elbows resting on the sash. Her head and bust showed in soft, warm colours against the dark interior of the room, above the brown painted window-sash, and the red hue of her skirt came through the panes below. The last time Hakki stopped he whistled softly, but she did not turn her head, and he went on without looking back again, switching the heads off the daisies by the footpath with his stick.

Her eyes were towards the manse. The upper part of its square, north gable rose white over the dark, heather covered, east spur of the hill, that here ran down between the manse and Taft and ended in the steep rocks of the shore. The gable was white, for the "harl" had been picked off in the spring by old John Jarmson and his helpers and the wall left for the wind and rain to clean down through the summer, so that it might be freshly pointed before winter came again. The kirk was to the left, a little nearer Taft. On the near side of the dark strip of heather was a low, turf dyke, the boundary at that spot between the glebe and Taft, almost hidden now from Inga's window by the corn of Taft across which waves of greenish-yellow light were being driven by the gentle breeze that had sprung up from the west as evening fell.

Nearer again was a small field of potatoes, its darker green making the oat field show more brightly out between it and the deep, brown heather just beyond. Inga sat musing for a long time. She was ill-pleased that she had shown her mother and Hakki too that she had been annoyed, for she was really more of a Bolt than of a Perk. She felt sure that the Perk side of the house would tease her afterwards about her evident desire to stand well with the minister, and this disturbed her, for, as she sat and thought, she knew that there had come that day into her heart a strange, new feeling that had never entered it before. She felt as if real life were just beginning for her, as if she had touched the hem of Fate's garment and the touch had thrilled her. She knew she was not thinking of Mr. Mann as minister at all, that the impression he had made upon her in that way had only led up to the moment when their eyes had met, that from that moment they had stood upon another plane. This almost frightened her at first, though Hakki's influence had strengthened in her her own feeling that she was as good as any of her neighbours high or low, and that her lineage as a Bolt was as old and honourable as could be wished, and much more so than that of many families that thought themselves the better class and happened now to own the land. When her eyes had met Mr. Mann's at parting, she had felt only that they two were equal, that no creed or social custom could disturb that fact, and she was sure he felt it also. So she was eager now to meet him again. This was not the first time she had been aware of her own power, but it was the very first time she had felt delight in the thought of using it. She had been aware of it slightly with Hakki, and completely with Bob Ertirson. But Hakki was always sarcastic and Bob was always humble. She rose with a sigh, closed the window, and, turning from it, began to undress. She took a peep at herself in the looking-glass that stood on the chest of drawers under the skylight, and smiled. After she had put on her nightgown she sat down on the front of her bed and, with her arms folded on her rounded bosom, looked through the window once again. A funny fancy came into her head. The white manse gable with its two windows, rising over the dark heather seemed to her like Sholma's solemn face looking at her, as she had often seen it, over the yard-dyke. With a little laugh, she jumped into bed. She had nearly fallen asleep when a wild yell sounded from the stairhead just outside her door. She sat up, startled. Then she remembered.

"My! It's only Uncle Jacob," she murmured, and lay down again.

CHAPTER III

BOB

"Conticuere omnes."—VIRGIL

NEXT Saturday afternoon Mr. Mann went out for his usual short walk. He turned, as was his wont, to the northwest, up the green slope at the foot of which stood Kirk and Manse, across the dark strip of heather, along below the corn of Hooll, up the steep footpath between the "rigs," and so on to the top of the hill behind old Magnus Sharp's house. As he walked, he repeated half aloud to himself bits of his sermon for the morrow. The theme was "Praise" again. He could not get beyond it.

There was a fine view from the top of the hill; but when he reached the top he was so taken up with his own thoughts that for a time he gave no heed to it. He stopped, however, and turned his eyes absently to the north-east and the entrance of the voe. He had chosen for his text the first clause in the first verse of the sixty-fifth Psalm. The fact of his physical position slowly forced itself upon his notice, but it was mingled with his spiritual reflections.

"Praise waiteth for Thee, O God, in Zion," he repeated aloud. He had ended his sermon by stating that the praise God wanted most was that of Man, that of the sole free agent to be found in all His universe. He felt that this still waited potentially in the world leavened by the Church, and he made that thought the basis of his earnest closing appeal. He felt that spiritually as well as physically he stood at that moment upon a hilltop, calling to his people to come up to the holy height and bask there in the glory. Then he remembered that last Sunday he had noticed two old men asleep. Three or four times the thought of it had pained him. There was, too, that little, unsatisfactory incident with Inga. That had been in his mind several times, but only vaguely. The two old men who had slept bulked more in his thoughts. But these things were trifles; he would put all right. He looked out over the landscape as it lay bathed in bright sunlight. Out on the blue sea at the entrance of the voe was a herring boat, coming in. She was coming slowly. The wind was from the west and very light. On the boat's brown mainsail he could see the splatch of white that, at the distance, stood for LK. and her number, and the other splatch of white that stood for the same thing upon her starboard bow. She had black topsides and a red bottom. The sun was full upon her. The sun was full on all he saw. He could see no shadows, for it was afternoon and he was looking from the west. If he had looked behind him he would have seen some; but there were none visible in front except his own, and he looked too high to see it. He did not think that there were shadows on the other side of everything he saw, that even the herring boat out there had a black shadow of her own, that she was coming up the voe fraught with what in such a world as this might come to be a tragedy.

He felt only that he stood spiritually as well as, at that moment, physically, above his people, and that it should be his task, his duty, his delight to lead them higher.

A black ewe with a white lamb by her side looked in curiously at him through the uneven bars of the rickety, old hillgate a little way behind him, while the lamb took advantage of its mother's preoccupation by trying to get an extra drink.

After a few minutes he turned down the hill again, passed along the yard-dyke of Hooll, round the corner of the byre, along in front of it and the barn, and reached the door of old Magnus' workshop which was standing open. He looked in. Magnus was sitting on his stool near the big window, in his blue shirtsleeves and leather apron, his grey head bare and bent towards the floor. He had just laid the boot he had been stitching up on the broad window sill, and was lifting his lapstone from the floor.

"Good day, Magnus," said Mr. Mann, entering.

Magnus raised his head till the light gleamed on his spectacles, making his small black eyes almost invisible, but they were looking sharply at the minister, who had not before come into the workshop though he had often saluted Magnus in passing or when they had chanced to meet outside.

"Yes, it's been a fine day, sir; bit I dont winder at it," said the old man in a decided tone, and seemingly taking the greeting more as a statement of fact than as a form of politeness. He began to hammer a piece of bend upon his lapstone.

"You don't wonder at it," said Mr. Mann with a slight smile, "how so, Magnus?"

"I sall tell you; I sall tell you"; returned Magnus, "bit ye'll set you doon first, edder here upo da window-sole or ower yondru upo da boy's stöl. I'm sory I hae no a shair to offer you."

"No, thank you," said Mr. Mann cheerily, "I'll just stand for this time. I'm on my way home, and I must call at the shop too. Well, how so, Magnus?"

Magnus ceased beating for a moment, and his spectacles, his little black eyes, his nose, and in fact the whole of his brown, wrinkled face peered up at Mr. Mann.

"Weel, ye see," said Magnus, "da Loard is hed a göd dael o practice at makkin days nu, an I dont winder 'at He turns oot a fine ean, nu an dan." He began to beat again. He was not in the habit of going to the kirk. Mr. Mann knew this well enough. It was for that reason he had come in along. He wished to lead the old man into other ways. He felt the old man's levity.

"Don't you think," he said, in a voice kindly but severe and with a troubled look in his dark eyes, "that it is very wrong of you to speak in such a way? Are you not afraid that God may punish you for your irreverence?"

"Me oonreverent!" said Magnus, hammering vigorously at his bend. "Na, na, sir; an as for poonishment, da Loard'll never pit Himsell aboot ta hairm a pör body laek me."

"This is worse and worse, Magnus," said Mr. Mann sadly, but with some little irritation, "and you have persisted so long, too, in stopping away from public worship."

"Public worship," echoed Magnus, stopping abruptly again, "Yea, it's public anoff; bit I dont know aboot da worship. Hoo mony o da folk, tink ye, goes dere ta worship? Da most o da lasses goes ta shaa aff dir bits o cloes, da most o da lads ta sit an glower at dem again, an da most o da aald folk becaase it's da custom ta go an dey're frichtend for what dir neeburs wid say if dey didna. Tink ye 'at da laek o Hansi Bolt wid bodder wi da kirk if it wisna for his shop? Not he, feth, sir. An as for me, I went ta da kirk reglar wance upun a time too; bit da aald body 'at wis afore you—rest his saal! he wis a göd, kind man tho nothin o a praecher—wis for ever grapplin wi texts 'at wis da same as guddiks (riddles). As I mony a time said, he wid lay a passage doon laek a shaef o coarn atween him an ean o da commentaators 'at he wis aye fechtin wi an dey wid turn to an wallop awey at it time aboot, till deevil a grain o sense wis left 'ithin it an dey wir raised a stoor o wirds 'at wis anoff ta blinnd a body. He keepit wis a whole winter sittin wi Job upun his middenhead, an anidder whole winter waanderin here an dere among da peerie (little) prophets, an what, can ye tell me, kent da laek o yon Naaum and Malakki aboot wis awa nort here in Shetland an dem dead thusans o years afore we wer boarn?"

"Probably more than you imagine, Magnus," said Mr. Mann quietly. He saw, however, that he would need to come oftener to Hooll. He did not get time to say more, for Magnus, who after his speech had looked through the big window, suddenly ejaculated,

"Yea, I toucht dat! Dere's Hansi's boat, da 'Inga,' comin in ta Da Point. I wis jöst tinkin at Bob Ertirson wid be comin haem dis Helly (Saturday to Monday). Hansi haes anidder Inga 'at Bob wid laek a hantle better ta be skipper o. So, so, wir Magni'll be wi him. Dis is a pair o Sundays böts ta Bob 'at I'm finishin even nu."

Through the open doorway Mr. Mann saw the herring boat gliding in towards a little cove among the black rocks of Da Point from which the dark strip of heather ran up between the glebe and Taft.

"Well, Magnus," said Mr. Mann, holding out his hand," I must be going now; but we must have a talk on church matters again." Magnus took his hand and shook it heartily, with a smile of mingled cynicism and good humour on his dried, old visage.

"Yea, yea, dat we sall," he said, "d'ill be nae want o taalk. Feth, I tink it's little else bit taalk aatagedder." Mr. Mann went out and walked slowly away, leaving Magnus chuckling to himself, as he gave a big knock on his lap-stone.

"Bi mi sang! I tink dat did him."

A young woman passed the window. Magnus glanced up and saw that it was Janny Gair, with a white handkerchief about her head, and a red one, in which half-a-dozen eggs were tied, in her left hand, and looking easier in her drab week day frock than she was wont to look on Sundays. She was in a hurry.

"So, so, my lamb," muttered Magnus with a smile, "I wis lippnin (expecting) yon. Du's makkin dy bit o aerrand ta da shop nu at du's awaar o Bob. Weel, weel; twa o you canna get him; bit ye'll see, my jewels, ye'll see."

Janny overtook Mr. Mann at the head of the steep "gaet" or footpath.

"It's a fine day, Janet," said he, in a somewhat absent tone.

"Yiss, sir, it's a very handsome day," said she, in her best English, and passed quickly down the path.

As soon as Bob had got his boat moored safely to the natural pier of rocks down at Da Point, he left the other men to snug things down, jumped ashore, and started for the shop of Taft, remarking as he went that he was "wantin a bit o tabacha" for himself.

"Du's in an almighty hurry for tobacco, boy," shouted Erti Gair, Janny's brother who had been "out West," after him, "I guess du better stop an fix up a bit before du tackles Taft." The rest grinned, but Magni Sharp gave Erti a slap between the shoulders that nearly sent him head first overboard.

"Shut di mooth, lad, an mind disell," said he, and Erti did so for the present.

Bob had on his big seaboots, covered with herring-scales from that morning's catch, his brown jersey, and his old slouch hat, once black, now greenish brown. But he had not seen Inga for six months, and he could not wait till after he had snugged the boat, gone home to Sætter, had a wash and change, and come back to the shop again. He knew, from Ann's last letter, that Inga had come home the week before. As he walked rapidly along the banks below the "rigs" of Taft, glancing every other moment at the house, he saw Janny Gair come down along the yard and go into the shop. She was the only customer in it when he reached it. Hansi and Inga were both in past the counter, but Inga had her back towards the door, for she was putting back a piece of printed cotton in its shelf. She turned as he entered, smiled, and instantly held out her hand to him.

"Du's welcome back, boy," she said. "What wy is du been sin Yöl?" Her easy manner to him always put Bob out. His heart was beating violently, though he seemed stolid enough till he spoke.

"Du's w-welcome back d-disell," he said, pressing her hand tenderly in his big, hard palm. He knew that his voice sounded rough and husky. He was at a loss for something more to say. Janny was watching them with all her might, and, in her eagerness to call Bob's attention to herself, she helped him out of his predicament, though at that moment he was wishing her at "Druntin" (Drontheim), being too good a soul to wish her farther. She held out her hand to Bob as if there was no necessity for his spending time on a mere acquaintance like Inga, when an intimate friend like herself was there.

"It's a plaesur to see dee hame again, boy," she said meaningly, while Inga went round the counter to weigh the hard sugar Janny wanted for her eggs. Bob shook hands with Janny, but his clear, blue eyes turned after Inga with the patient, pleading look they always had when she was by.

"Ar ye aa weel at Vatster?" he grunted out.

Hansi rose from the desk at the window where he had been writing and came forward.

"Weel, boy, what news wi dee?" he asked heartily; "what ar ye don dis week?" Bob's devotion had a profitable side to it.

"We hed fifty cran on Wadnsdy, an aboot forty cran dis moarnin," answered Bob, merely glancing at Hansi as he shook hands with him, and then fixing his eyes on Inga again. He thought she had never looked prettier than she did now. The light from the window and from the open door was full upon her where she stood bareheaded, in her pink print dress, weighing the sugar. It seemed to Bob that no girl in the world could be more beautiful. While she stood there, footsteps sounded outside and a shadow from the doorway fell upon her. It was Mr. Mann who entered. She had been thinking of him through the week, but they had never met. Bob noticed that she gave a little start. Mr. Mann's thoughts were busy with old

Magnus' words. He did not seem to see her though she was right before him, till after he had greeted Hansi; then he turned to her and the others. Bob saw her manner was not quite so easy now; but Janny did not for she had her back to Inga. Mr. Mann began to speak to Bob about the fishing. Bob glanced at him and thought how rough and dirty he himself must look beside him. He wished that he had waited and gone home before coming to the shop. Janny had expected that he would do this and had made an errand east to the shop on the chance of walking home with him and having him to herself a while before Inga, and so she was disappointed now and she took her sugar and left the shop, smiling sweetly to Bob, however, as she went and saying,

"So, boy, we'll see dee at Vatster da moarn." Bob did not answer her; but as he answered Mr. Mann he thought how hoarse and gruff his own voice was, and what a blockhead he had been to come like this, in his coarse jersey, his old wreck of a hat, and his great sea-boots, and with the strong smell of the fishing boat about him. He felt that he must get away as fast as possible. He turned to Inga, who had come round the counter again. He saw her manner was quite easy now, but he did not know that it was so because she was feeling piqued at Mr. Mann for seeming so unconscious of her presence.

"Will du gie me a wharter o pound o tabacha wi di haand, lass?" he said, and Inga knew well enough that he was agitated. He hoped her hand would touch his when she gave him the tobacco. She gave it to him, and his hope was realised. But he lingered still.

"I tink I'll tak a haaf a pound o conversation sweeties," he said. As Inga weighed them, he saw it would be ridiculous for him to take them with him now, for he was going to the boat again. He muttered something about getting it at night, and Inga set the paper bag aside for him. His eyes were on her face. There was no way for him to know that she had picked out from the box a pink sweet shaped like a heart with the two words, "Take it," printed red upon it, and that she kept it hidden in her hand.

"Ye'll come in alang da hoose a moment, sir," said Hansi to Mr. Mann. "Da wife'll no be plaesed if I lat you go awa withoot her seein you." Mr. Mann objected quietly, but Hansi overruled him.

"Rin in, lass, an tell di midder 'at da minister is comin in alang," said Hansi, knowing what would happen if he brought in any person of importance without timely warning.

"I'd like an ounce of cut tobacco, if you please," said Mr. Mann. Inga turned to get it for him before going into the house, for she was anxious to let her hand touch his and notice its effect; her vanity was hurt at his complete indifference. But Hansi said,

"I'll get it. Rin du in, Inga," and she had to do so. As she moved past Mr. Mann, who stood close to the counter door, she dropped the pink, heart-shaped sweet neatly into his jacket pocket, as she thought. She felt forced to play this trick upon him, for she almost always acted instantly, and therefore inconsiderately, whenever she was irritated. Next moment she was sorry, nearly frightened at what she had done. It had changed suddenly from trifling trick to inexcusable impudence in her mind. Last Sunday she had felt she was his equal, and her thoughts had been quite serious, though somewhat vague. But now the notion of the social difference between them, that notion in which she had been so carefully reared, especially by Willa, and by which she had been ruled till Hakki came, occurred to her so strongly that she blushed for shame. What had she done? The man was really a perfect stranger to her, though her father had known his father intimately. She had been acting on a little incident that might or might not have been the faint beginning of a tacit understanding of equality; but that incident Mr. Mann seemed to have quite forgotten. What was he to think when he had guessed? She was glad his back was to her now. But Bob's blue eyes were fixed upon her and a strange look was in them. She knew that he must see her blushing, but he could not know the reason, and for him, at any rate, she did not care. Her mood changed instantly again, and, with a nervous, but defiant, little laugh, she hurried out.

Mr. Mann turned again to speak to Bob while Hansi was getting his tobacco, and the pink heart, which had not gone into the pocket but had been caught by the lid, dropped at that moment to the floor. Bob stooped, and picked it up. He had been mentally contrasting his bogie-roll with Mr. Mann's cut-cavendish, but Inga's blush had set him thinking in a harder way, and now he slipped the sweet into his trousers' pocket and kept thinking harder still. For three years he had loved Inga madly, though she had not encouraged him except by letting him alone, to come about the house as often as he pleased and take his chance of seeing her. When he had gone to sea at fifteen, she had been a little girl of eleven. When, after five years sailing, he had taken a run home one winter, he had found her an extremely pretty maiden of sixteen, and so had found it very hard to go away again. He was always in earnest, had simple, straightforward ideas, and was afraid of nothing on earth except Inga. His father, Jeems Ertirson, the kirk elder, had named him after the laird, for Jeems, with his easy going disposition and his good croft at Sætter, was a man always carefully respectful to "the powers that be." Bob had been strictly trained from infancy to duly honour his supposed superiors, and, as a man, he stuck still to the precept, for it suited his own nature. That pink sweet fairly staggered him. He had read the words upon it as he picked it up. In spite of his apparent stolidness his wits were quick. Suspicion was the rack on which he was continually torturing himself. Inga's ease of manner to him kept him always on it, for he never felt that he was getting any nearer to her. Now he had got a shock. Inga had always seemed to his enamoured eyes a sensible and modest girl, though sometimes rather too light hearted for the pain he felt.

Many a night in the course of the past winter and spring he had come to Taft to hear if possible some news of Inga for she would not let him write to her, and at such times Willa had, with certain pleasure to herself, for she thought he was hardly good enough for Inga, told him bits of news from Inga's letters, which bits were usually about the jolly time that she was having and the tricks she had been playing on the Fetlar lads that came about her uncle's house. But this trick was another matter. He could not help feeling that Inga had tried to do a silly and impudent thing, and that his own respect for her had got a blow. For six months he had never seen her, or heard directly from her, and this was what had happened now when, full of love and longing, he had hurried to her. Jealousy was hardly present yet. He regarded Inga as socially his equal, and Mr. Mann as socially superior to them both, and he could not think seriously of anything between them. He did not know about the look that Mr. Mann and Inga had exchanged the previous Sunday, and what might possibly grow from it in the future, a look that had declared to both of them that they were equal. Mr. Mann's manner was so grave and earnest; but again, Bob did not know that he was standing thinking of old Magnus Sharp and of what kind of parish this was he had got to minister to in spiritual concerns. Bob thought of Inga's blush and of the defiant, little laugh that followed it immediately. He had grown angry. He would wait till she came back into the shop again, and Hansi took the minister into the house, then he and Inga would be left alone together.

Inga had just come back into the shop and was standing out past the counter between Bob and Mr. Mann, when Jacob, Hansi's brother who was crazy, came to the door and looked in with a solemn grin on his rather broad, bristly, red face, out of which both his big blue eyes stared at you with a puzzled, very sad expression, like those of a man who waits for help that never comes. On his head he wore an old, hard felt hat with a band of "simmind" or straw rope about it, and he had his jacket on inside out for he thought that it was cooler so, while on his feet he had a pair of red "rivlins," cowhide sandals, with white spots upon them, and with the right leg of his trousers turned up nearly to his knee.

"Nu, nu," he said, pointing in at them with the remains of an old staff he carried in his hand, "Na, na. Twa lads, wan lass. No good. He, he! Kiss an 'gree."

For a moment they all stood silent, then Hansi took Mr. Mann into the house and Jacob slowly followed them, for he had taken a strong fancy to the minister.

Bob turned to Inga suddenly as soon as they were gone. She had gone in past the counter.

"I never toucht du wis a föl till nu," he said bitterly and with great effort, for his fear of her was struggling with his anger. He held the pink sweet out towards her in his open hand. She looked at it. He saw her face grow fiery red.

Then she laughed, as she had done before. She grew at once cool again.

"I never asked dee for di touchts," she said, with cutting calmness. "Du'll better keep dem till I dö." For a little, Bob stood struggling with himself, then all at once he turned on his heel and strode out of the shop.

CHAPTER IV

"JOHNSMAS FLOOERS"

"Fata obstant."—VIRGIL

BOB did not trouble old Magnus for his new Sunday boots that night. As he walked west over towards Sætter with Erti Gair he never once spoke, and Erti, knowing well enough that Bob was angry, thought it wisest to be silent too. When they got to the end of the loch on the east shore of which Vatster lay, they parted. As Bob turned up towards Sætter, which lay a bit up the steep slope of the hill west of the loch, he noticed Janny and Ann and a red cow by the loch shore at the foot of the Vatster "rigs." The lasses were looking for something on the ground. They did not know that Bob had passed till Erti reached them. Janny was vexed, for she had seen them coming over Da Aest Hill and had come down from the house in order to meet them; but just afterwards she had seen Ann coming down from Sætter, and when Ann got to her they had begun to look for "Johnsmas Flooers." They were each choosing the best two bits of ribwort they could find, for it was St. John's Eve. The sun was sinking behind the hills to the north-west, and half the brown, north gable of the house at Sætter was lighted up. The north end of the loch lay in deep shadow.

Bob passed from the sunlit grass at the loch's south end into the shadow of the hill and tramped doggedly up towards Sætter. He felt as if everything was going from sunshine to shadow. He hardly looked at their three cows, a red and white one, an ashey brown one, and a black one with a white face, which were tethered on the lea ground below the corn, and which Ann had come down to fetch up to the byre when she had noticed Janny by the loch. The red and white cow and the ashey Brown one looked steadily at Bob for a little and then began quietly to eat again as if there was no need of making a fuss even though Bob had come home again; but the black one with the white face, still called "sholmit" or helmeted, just as she would have been in the old Norse time, looked after him sadly and gave a little low when he had passed. She was the one he usually petted most, because she was the daughter of the Taft "Sholma." When he was near the house his little black-and-tan collie Berry came springing about him with every sign of joy, but Berry soon found out that he had better be quiet, and he went meekly in at the house door at Bob's heel. His mother was in the "but-end" getting supper ready, and Jeems was sitting on the "restin-shair," a long wooden seat with back and arms, that stood across the window. Jeems was reading his old, big print Bible, as was his wont on Saturday nights.

Both he and Mary welcomed Bob without making much ado. Mary was a quiet body, somewhat past middle age, with a kindly face and a figure very short and bulky. She was old John Jarmson's sister, and so came of a quaint and placid family.

"Weel boy, we're blyde ta see dee," she said gently and went on setting up the peats about the fire.

Bob sat down on the resting-chair beside his father without speaking and for a few minutes looked fixedly at the fire-flame leaping up about the pot. Then Jeems said quietly, in his usual measured tones,

"Sall I draa aff dy böts, boy?" He laid down his book.

"Yea, dat ye can," Bob answered gruffly. As soon as the big boots were off, he stuck his feet into a pair of clogs that stood below the resting-chair, and rose.

"Here's dee a pair o dry socks," said Mary, pulling them down from the "raep" or line that ran across the room. Bob took them from her without a word and went upstairs. The old folk saw that something was amiss, but they said nothing, even to each other.

His room was a little place with a lifting skylight, right above the "but-end," the living room of the cottage. It took up only part of the space above, for the "but-fire" sent its smoke up past the side of it and out, though not invariably, through a round hole in the thatched roof. It was a cosy little place even in winter, for the "but-fire" was nearly in the middle of the earthen floor below. Bob had lined it all with wood and fitted it up with many little shelves and lockers, for he was good at joinerwork. He had done this the first winter he came home. He had begun to it as soon as he had fallen in love with Inga and had settled that he would stay home a while. If Inga had then given him the slightest hope, he would have gone away again at once, in order to get on as fast as possible at sea. But she did not. That was three years ago and he was waiting still. He felt now, as he had felt all along, that it was useless for him to go away without some hope of winning Inga, for without that hope he had no wish whatever to get higher in a worldly way than he was now. He asked himself now, as he had done often before and sometimes bitterly, what the end would be.

"God onnly knows," he muttered to himself in answer, as he sat down on his chest lid and hauled his jersey off over his head. After he had had a wash and changed his clothes, he stood for a while looking out through the skylight, which was on a level with his chin, and was wide open. The afterglow from the northwest lay over the whole landscape. It was on the brown hills across the quiet voe, two miles away, and on the mile of land that lay between Bob and the shore. Below him and a little to the left the loch lay calm in shadow with the Gair's croft nestling on its farther side, the thin smoke curling up from the "but-lum," and Janny leading the red cow into the byre. To the right Da Wast Hill, on which Sætter was, sent out a gentle slope to the north-east, on which lay old John Jarmson's croft, Da Krö, so called because the sheepfold used by the whole neighbourhood was just behind it, outside the hill-dyke. Away to the south-east, close by the shore and at the end of the green valley through which a small burn ran down from the loch, stood the laird's house, always called "Da Ha," although it had another name. The afterglow was on it. On the shoulder of Da Aest Hill, right opposite to Sætter, the white Schoolhouse stood out in the soft, evening light, and Bob could see a figure which he knew was Hakki's, leaning over the low garden wall. To the right a bit, the Manse roof and the Kirk roof showed above the slope that formed the foot of Da Aest Hill towards the south. They looked dark against the sea. But Bob's eyes rested only for a moment on any of these points; for, through a hollow in the slope below the Schoolhouse, the south chimneytop of Taft and the upper half of

Inga's window were in sight. He gazed so fixedly at that spot, three-quarters of a mile away, that one might easily have thought it was the first time he had noticed that it could be seen. The shadow of Da Aest Hill was over Taft. There was only the grey gable with the dark, little opening on it in sight; but he stood and gazed.

After a while he turned and lifted from the locker of his chest a cabinet photograph which he held up to the skylight. It was not one of Inga, at least not one of Inga by herself, for she had always refused to give him that in case he should mistake its meaning. It was a group of about forty school children, with Inga standing by Lowra Sharp's side up at the back. She was very small in the picture, but Bob had cut a little, oblong slit in a small piece of cardboard, and when he placed this on the photograph he had a tiny photograph of Inga by herself at which he often looked through a big reading-glass that had once magnified the Scriptures for his father's mother, Synnie Jeemson, who lay now, with her old eyes closed for ever, in the kirkyard by the voe. While he stood looking so, and thinking over what had come and gone since he with his small feet bare and brown had waded in the little burn below the School, chasing the tiny speckled trout that darted here and there in the still, sunlit pools, he heard footsteps coming up the path towards the house, and, glancing out, saw it was his sister Jeanie, who had run up from the Ha to spend an hour or two now he was come. He heard her calling laughingly to Ann, who was just coming from the byre, and asking if she had plucked any "Johnsmas Flooers." His mother's voice sounded from the foot of the stair—

"Will du come doon ta dy supper, boy?" He put the photograph back carefully into his trunk again, and, locking it, went downstairs thinking of the "Johnsmas Flooers," wondering at himself for doing so. After supper a good while he walked down the dale a bit with Jeanie on her way back to the Ha, and as he came up slowly again towards Sætter he plucked two bits of ribwort and took them with him to his room. Before going to bed he picked the minute, creamy blades from the dark heads, and naming one stalk "Inga" and the other "Bob," laid them down in his trunk beside the photograph. As soon as he awoke next morning he rose and looked at them with an anxiety of which he almost felt ashamed. But his giving way to this small bit of superstition had not helped him much. The tiny blades had not grown on again to any great extent. They were just visible and so the hope they had to give was very small and far away. He wondered whether he should go to the kirk that day or not; but, after breakfast, habit and his own naturally earnest disposition sent him out, and with them was the feeling that he must see Inga every time that this was possible, whatever might come of it all. The day was beautifully fresh and bright as the day before had been; but he felt out of tune with the freshness and the brightness of it, and especially with its sickening peacefulness when he was troubled so. He held along the hill and round the north end of the loch for he saw Janny Gair and Erti out before their door at Vatster and he did not wish to meet them. When he had gone through the hill gate at the back of Hooll and had got to the top of the hill he stood there looking down on Taft. He meant to go in along Hooll for Magni Sharp. He heard footsteps at the corner of the house and saw Magni's head and shoulders passing along the top of the yard-dyke. Magni saw him and came up towards him, smoking and humming a tune, his dog Starry jumping excitedly about him. Berry had not risked following Bob. Bob wished he was as light of heart as Magni seemed; but he did not know that Magni understood him far better than he yet understood Magni. They sat down together on the heather, Bob with his blue eyes fixed on Inga's skylight in the roof of Taft, while Magni with his brown eyes watched him in a way that might have told Bob something, had he noticed it.

"Whar's dy pipe, boy?" said Magni. "Is du not goin ta hae a smok? It's a while ta kirk time yit."

Bob drew from his pocket a sealskin tobacco pouch, in which was a part of the twist he had bought from Inga. It seemed to him he felt the touch of her hand on his again, as he began to cut a pipeful. They sat and smoked in silence, Bob's eyes only once or twice leaving the skylight, to glance down at his herring boat, the mast of which stood up yellow in the bright sunlight among the black rocks of Da Point, while he wondered whether she was all the "Inga" he would ever have. After a while he saw the Bolts come out from Taft, and his heart jumped as he caught sight of Inga. They started to move slowly towards the kirk. Bob and Magni rose and began to saunter down the hill, leaving Starry sitting disconsolate on the heather till all at once he recollected that the hens were in the yard, and being lax in his observance of the Sunday, jumped the dyke and began sportively to chase them round and round until their screams and scolding brought Lowra from the house when he desisted, and, crawling towards her on his stomach with his tail wagging somewhat hopefully, tried to explain that it was all in fun. Lowra warmed his ear with the flat of her hand and ordered him into the house, where he took refuge under the resting-chair, on which old Magnus was sitting smoking, and, sticking his nose from below it, tried to lick the old man's hand.

"Weel, Starry," said Magnus, patting him, "what's dis nu?" Du aye rins ta me wi dy bits o troubles. So, so; pör ting, pör ting." Lowra came in too.

"Faeder," she said with emphasis, "it's you 'at maks a föl o da dug. He's been shaestin da hens roond an roond da yard, an nu ye sit an clap him."

"O, du villan," she added, shaking her fist at Starry, "if I catch dee döin da laek again." Starry withdrew his nose from old Magnus' hand and retired altogether under the resting-chair.

"Haddi tongue, lass," said Magnus, looking at Lowra with the sarcastic pucker on his face, "da pör bit o whalp is not a kirk member, an du needna be sae particwilar aboot his conduck upo da Sunday. Be raisonable wi da pör, spaechless anamal." Lowra flounced into the "ben" room, and snatching her hat from the top of the chest of drawers, she put it on and started after Bob and Magni. The three overtook the Bolts. Bob would have liked to let Inga and her folk keep in front, but Magni and Lowra went up to them and he had to do so too. His eyes met Inga's and he felt that she was fairly changed. There was in her look a gentleness towards him he had never seen before. His heart gave even a greater jump than it had given on the hilltop when he had seen her leave the house. Then he felt that it was only foolish of him to believe himself so fortunate.

When they reached the kirk door, the Bolts and Lowra went right in, but Bob and Magni stopped among the group that usually gathered there, outside, where they were free to talk of earthly things, and waited till the minister went in. Most of them hailed Bob and Magni. Erti

Gair, who was standing on the doorstep, merely said,

"Wal, boys," and relapsed into silence. He had seen Bob go round the north end of the loch and had not liked it. He had kept a keen eye on Inga as she had come up and gone into the kirk. He was got up in his best style. His hard felt hat was tipped forward over his pointed nose and his sly, gray eyes looked out sharply from the shadow, while his thin, somewhat sallow face with its black moustache and goatee beard had a sort of "Wal, I'm darned" expression always on it. He wore a navy blue suit, an almost white shirt front and cuffs, a red tie, and silver studs and sleevelinks with raised anchors on them. Bob noticed his keen glance at Inga, but this did not make him feel worse than he was, for he thought Erti such a fool. Magni saw it too, though Magni never seemed to notice anything, and last night's slap on Erti's back had something to do with it also. Erti's father, Aald Erti, was standing by his side, just below the step. The neighbours called him

Aald Erti to distinguish him from his polished son, whom they called Young Erti when they used his name, but who was much more widely known throughout the parish by his title of "Da Yenky," a title which he rather liked than otherwise, for he felt it was a public tribute to his parts, as well as a continual reminder to the limpets who had never left their native Rock that this man had been "west." Aald Erti was very plainly an earlier, leather-bound edition of the son. His face was brown and thin. He had the sly gray eye that was repeated in Young Erti. Of late he had grown used to dressing himself up in "Da Yenky's" disused suits, and so instead of looking like a pretty fairly well-off crofter body as he was, he had a kind of "reduced circumstances" air about him, and it would have been a puzzle to a stranger to say what he was, at the first glance. One could, however, see quite well that he too had been "west," but not so far "west" as his son. He never came to the kirk unless Young Erti was at home, when he would come fussing to the sacred edifice at

Erti's side, and pause till the last moment at the door to give the neighbours the full benefit of the imposing scene. Like his son, he used the English tongue, with variations.

"Good mornin, boys," said Aald Erti jerkily, shaking hands with Bob and Magni, and especially with Bob, for he knew well his daughter Janny's leaning. Then old John Jarmson came up, with his left hand as usual on the back of his blue pilot coat.

"Weel, my Bob, what news?" he said, as they shook hands.

"No muckle, uncle, what news wi yoursell?" returned Bob.

"I'm tinkin du got twartree herrin da last week," said old John. "It wis a mercy; it wis a mercy."

"Yea, we hed a few," said Bob. "He's been very fine wadder.

"Prinncipal, boy, prinncipal; he's raelly been prinncipal wadder for da herrin," said old John, passing on into the kirk, and mopping his brow with his red cotton handkerchief as he went.

"Yes, it's relly very necessitous wedder," said Aald Erti, with a dignified air; "yes, very necessitous, both for da fishing an so for da crops."

"Tink ye?" said Magni, winking at Bob. "Feth, I tink he's redder overly wi hot nu."

"Well, even allowin that," said Aald Erti, "it's still very necessitous, an very handsome wedder." It was evidently from him that Janny took her choicest bits of English.

"Dis ain't to be called hot," said Young Erti from the doorstep, with a touch of contempt not unmixed with pity in his tone. "I guess you fellows don't exackly know what hot is. I seen a man's hair sweed [singed] right clean off his head with hot wan time out in the States."

"Yes," said Aald Erti, jerkily, "I seen the very same."

"No faeder," said Young Erti decidedly, "I guess not. You was only in Canady, wasn't you? Canady ain't no good." Aald Erti collapsed.

Mr. Mann came from the vestry and passed into the kirk, and all the others went in after him.

All through the service Bob sat thinking of that look in Inga's eyes. He could not understand it, but the thought of it was sweet to him in spite of all his doubts. Had he known the feeling that led actually to it, it would have pained him more than he had yet been pained.

He and Magni sat in a sideseat a little farther back than Inga's was, and her head was luckily, or otherwise, in sight above the yellow locks of "peerie" Oli Jarmson, old John Jarmson's youngest grandson. He sat glancing at her every other moment, and, at each glance, he felt that a new chain was fastening his heart to hers more strongly than before; but what of hers to his? If, after all, that silly bit of flower divination meant that there was hope; if, after all, it meant the very opposite; what then? He felt that, if he had to lose her finally, it would be better for him not to look at her so often now; but he could not get his eyes away, for he felt next instant that, if this were so, he must look oftener still. He had no will when she was by. Last night had been the very first time he had yet strained at his cable. He thought he had nearly broken it. But her look to-day had quenched the smouldering remnants of his anger at her foolishness, and he was on the rack of hope and jealousy again. He leaned his elbow on the seatback and his cheek upon his hand, and sat and looked at her more fixedly than he had done. The sermon had begun. At times he felt she was looking too intently towards the pulpit. Then he felt that other young men in the kirk were looking too intently towards her pew. He was right in this, for one of them was sitting in the seat beside him, though he did not know as yet. He saw that Hakki, who had come in late, was always looking down at Inga.

Mr. Mann was eloquent as usual, and at moments Bob was conscious of this fact and felt assured in his belief that Inga could not possibly have serious thoughts of being able to get *him.* He felt glad, now he was calmer, that nothing had come of her foolish trick. It stung him still to think of it. But there was no girl like her in the place, he thought. What if she really had such serious notions? Jeanie had told him that the laird's daughter was expected home. Yes, there would be some sense in it, if *she* should think herself a match for Mr. Mann. But Mr. Mann was young, as he was. Suppose he should fall in love with Inga. This last thought angered him. He felt that Mr. Mann would have no right to do so. But he remembered that the Bolts were better off than they appeared, that Hansi Bolt was really pretty rich although he sometimes went about in a sleeved waistcoat and even rubbed the flour and oatmeal from his hands upon the back part of his trousers. Perhaps Mr. Mann, like many other men and ministers that he had known about, might think of solid things like these when coupled with a lass like Inga, and Inga could behave, if she but cared to do so, at least as well as Mrs. Black and in some ways a very great deal better. Bob felt a bitter feeling rising in him against Mr. Mann, a bitter feeling that to his simple, honest nature seemed quite shameful as he thought of it, for he knew well enough that it had nothing but his own suspicious imagination as a basis to it yet. Again he thought of Inga's look and felt a thrill of hope.

He tried to listen now to the remainder of the sermon; but he was not in any mood for "Praise" which was its constant burden, and his eyes soon wandered back to Inga's head.

While Hansi and his father were scooping up the coppers with their two long wooden ladles, or "skaapnets" as Magni Sharp, with something of his father's jocular irreverence, usually called them, Bob saw that Mr. Mann was looking straight at Inga. He was almost certain of it, though he told himself that he might easily be making a mistake about it. He did not take part in the singing of the closing psalm. He was glad when the benediction was pronounced, and all was done.

As he passed with Magni slowly out the aisle, Inga was right behind him.

"We'll shörly see dee aest at Taft da nicht," she said in a low tone when they were near the door, and he was so surprised that he said, "Yea," as if he had been dreaming.

CHAPTER V

HAKKI

"The thoughts of youth are long, long thoughts."—H. W. LONGFELLOW

IT was about three o'clock in the afternoon when Bob came east to Taft. Inga had, of course, felt sure that he would come, for it was the very first time she had asked him even indirectly. She could scarcely understand herself why she had done so. The look of almost gentleness that she had given him that morning had not been born of pity but of pride. His sudden anger of the night before had made her angry too; but when he had stalked from the shop and she had stood and watched him striding down towards the herring-boat as if he felt that he had too long wasted love upon a worthless thing, her vanity had certainly been sorely wounded. He had always been so humble and obedient, so fairly in her power. She had not known till then how much the losing of his love might mean to her, not to her heart, but to her general satisfaction with herself. Everybody in the place knew how things stood, that Bob was actually her slave; but now he had rebelled and run away. This would be sweet to Janny Gair and to more folk than Janny. She would not let herself be laughed at by them. She would bring Bob back. So she had given Bob a look and those few words and he had come.

Hansi and Hakki had not gone into the yard to smoke; but they were sitting smoking in the parlour, the floor of which was covered with linoleum, on which Hansi sometimes spat in moments of forgetfulness, to be at once reproved and once more warned by his wife and Inga, who would remind him somewhat sharply of the earthenware spitoon beside his chair, when he would check himself so far as to spit next into the fire. Willa, with her volume of the "Christian Treasury," was sitting on the bulky, haircloth sofa, that stood across the window like a higher form of "restin-shair." They all greeted Bob in pretty much the same old way. Willa merely glanced up for a moment from her book and said,

"Hoo is du, boy, an what wy is your folk?" Then she went on with her laborious search for truth among the mutilated remnants of the polysyllables that she was murdering. Bob thought that Hakki was a little drier in his manner than was usual; but Hakki had a way of sometimes seeming rather dry, and Bob was thinking more of Inga's manner to him than of any other body's. Inga drew in one of the best chairs for him, and he noticed with a thrill that she herself sat down on one that he had made. He felt that she meant him to notice this.

After a little, Willa laid her book down in the window at her back, and said, with a very holy air, “Yun wis a winderfil discoorse ‘at we got frae Mester Mann da day.”

“Yea, dat it wis,” assented Hansi in the tone of one who knew his part and could respond mechanically; then he added with more interest, “an we hed a braa collection. Dis fine wadder brings da folk oot.” He aimed a little tobacco juice carelessly at the fire, and struck the shining fender.

“Faeder!” said Inga, warningly.

“Hoots, lass,” said Hansi, with a strong pull at his pipe, “I toucht I wis spittin i da aess [ashes].”

“Yea, less!” said Willa, with a sanctified sigh, “it taks fine wadder to bring dem oot nu. I’ my young days we toucht very little aboot da wadder.”

“Yes,” said Hakki, with a smile, “but the lasses have fine hats and bonnets to look after now.”

"Yea, my lamb," said Willa, with another sigh, "da world is aaful nu wi venity an foolichness." Then she added eagerly, for this topic had reminded her,

"Pat du my new bonnet inta da box, Inga?" When this was settled she reverted to the sermon, and Bob sat and wondered how Hakki could have heard so much of it, as it seemed he had done, and yet have looked so often down at Inga. Inga did not say very much; but nearly every time she spoke she contradicted Hakki, who at last got rather nettled. Then Hansi, who saw most things pretty clearly, rose from his chair, and said,

"Boys, I tink we'll go up inta da yard an finish wir smok. It's gettin very close in here."

Inga looked at Bob.

"Lat du dem twa go, Bob," she said, "du's never heard ony o my Fetlar news yet." Bob kept his seat, and Hakki followed Hansi out, with a peculiar look upon his face.

Willa took up her book again, and Inga, with her old, lighthearted manner, began telling Bob at once, some, but only some, of the incidents of her long stay in Fetlar. Bob, with his eyes fixed on her face, sat listening in a kind of dream from which he was awakened now and then as he remembered some of those small bits from Inga's letters that Willa had read to him in the winter. But Inga's voice and the bright glance of her deep, blue eyes, and, more than all, her nearness to him now and her new kindliness bewitched him into slavery again. He sat there, having a wide smile, like that which some men have when they are partially drunk, upon his face; and Hakki sat out in the yard and smoked, with a puzzled, angry look on his. After tea, Hakki left Taft in spite of all objections from the others and went home.

In the evening, Bob went down with Inga to fetch up the cows, and he tied them in the byre when she was done with milking them. When he was leaving after supper, she came out to the door with him. The night, like that of last

Sunday, was calm and beautiful. There was no sound but the occasional puff-fuff of a "nisik" (porpoise) passing in the voe. Inga drew the house-door close to after her. Bob was in a sweet tremble of excitement, for it was the first time she had come out to the door with him. He stood silent, looking at her in the rich, summer twilight. The thought that she with all the loveliness he saw in her might yet be his made him feel dizzy and quite stupid. He longed to seize her in his arms and press her to him; but his fear of her had come again, and he only stood there looking at her silently, his whole heart in his eyes. He felt he could linger near her, thus, for ever. Then all at once she said, with a little laugh and holding out her hand,

"So, göd nicht to dee, boy." She had been wont to let her hand lie passively in his; but now he shivered with delight as he felt that she gave a gentle, answering pressure to his warm clasp. Next moment, she had run into the house.

Bob slowly left the spot, and, as he crossed the valley on his way to Sætter, he saw the mist beginning to creep softly down between the dark hills to the north.

Inga sat at her window for a little looking out at Bob's retreating figure and at the white gable rising over the brown strip of heather. She was almost sorry now. She had brought Bob back, only to realise how fearfully he was in earnest, and to feel that she had for the first time really trifled with him, that is, wilfully deceived him. She tried to tell herself that it was only friendship that had made her say those few soft words to Bob that morning, those words that had brought him to Taft when he was likely for the very first time in his life to stop away. But she knew this was false, and she felt sure that Hakki had somehow been conscious of it and had despised her for it. She told herself she did not care what Hakki thought, but she knew better. She heard a shuffling noise beneath the window, and saw her uncle Jacob come round the corner of the house. For a little he stood looking after Bob's quickly disappearing figure on the shoulder of the hill, then he pointed after it with his imperfect staff and spat upon the ground, muttering angrily to himself the while. Inga knew his reason, and her thoughts grew still more troublesome. Jacob shuffled back into the kitchen, where he passed most of his time asleep in a great, straw-padded, wooden chair. Inga felt again, as she had felt last Sunday night, that Fate was coming near and touching her, that it had really now begun to feel about her life, like one of those vast octopi about which she had often heard her father and the men who went down to the sea in boats speak fearfully. She had been lighthearted since she was a child; but she saw that this could not help her now with real life beginning for her. She wished that she had been a bird, or some free thing, outside of human life, then she smiled at her own fancy, and immediately afterwards wished that Bob had not come home the winter that he did. She had never wished that before. She knew she never would have wished it but for what she had just done, for till that day she had not made herself a part of it at all. She looked across at the white gable with its two dark windows, and felt piqued at Mr. Mann again for seeming to ignore her in the shop. But he had looked at her in church. She heard her father moving about downstairs, shutting the doors, and Jacob shuffling after him. She rose and closed her window. As she did so, it seemed to her that she saw someone standing looking out through the west window on the white Manse gable; but she could not be sure. She thought, in a half troubled way, that Bob would be off early in the morning, to feast himself for a whole week upon the false belief of her changed feelings to him, and, for a moment, she wished that he could have stayed till she had put things back to their old way. She was so ignorant of life, as yet, that she thought this was possible. But she remembered Janny. Then her mind darted back again and she hoped Mr. Mann would come to Taft to-morrow. When she had undressed she sat a while upon the bed, her arms crossed on her full bosom, and looked out from the darkened room at that white gable looming through the summer twilight. Then she lay down, and, for the first time she remembered, could not get soon asleep for disagreeable thoughts.

It was Mr. Mann that she had dimly seen. He was standing in his bedroom window looking at the bright glow in the northern sky above the bank of mist that was now stealing slowly over Hooll. It seemed to him a picture of Eternity and Time, and he made a mental note of it for future use. But he was somewhat ill at ease. He had taken two or three turns round the room and had stopped once more at the window. He did not look at Taft at first. He was doing what he called his catechetics. He was questioning himself as to the progress of his work. Preaching was so novel to him yet and so attractive that he preached even to himself.

"It is the living word," he said aloud, "that flies abroad, that is the seedgrain of the Gospel. Christ sent His heralds out to teach all nations, to preach to them in short. The Gospel is not, and never can be, only a cold code of morals, a kind of `guide to unobjectionable conduct,' a handbook of etiquette for the Soul. No; it is a word of fire, a word filled with the Holy Ghost, a word of life flung out by God's own Son, to palpitate for ever on the air of Time till the elect of God are gathered in. Christ's resurrection is the proof of this. 'It is finished!' What is that It? Is that a dying good man's sentiment of satisfaction with his life? No, no; for ever, no! 'I have fought a good fight,' that is the apostle's formula, and there is no tremendous mystery suggested. Yes, I have preached that word of fire; but what of its result? How can men sleep? Why does not every soul that hears me thrill with eager interest? This is life or death, the mighty issues of Eternity. What is this apathy but a temptation from the Enemy of souls? But if this is all at the beginning of my ministry, what will it be when ears have grown accustomed to my words and their first interest is dulled? No, with the help of God, I will not spare. The world has never yet been roused but by a Cry. The pulpit is not all, however. No, I must get nearer to my people. The few who sleep in church will be awake at home. That old Magnus Sharp has need of me."

At the thought of old Magnus he grew silent, and stood for a little thinking, his fingers on his brow. Then Inga's deep blue eyes rose up before him and seemed looking into his. Yes, the elder's daughter Inga was one who listened, one who drank in every word. Her eager look had cheered him on the previous Sunday. He had felt the subtle sympathy of a pure young girl's soul. But what was that, that had come with it? Why had he felt that they were something more than only minister and hearer? What could there be in this? He saw nothing but the possibility of a true friendship, a spiritual sympathy that would be helpful to them both. Yes, he would step over to Taft to-morrow and ask her to take a class in the Sunday school. From her he passed to Hakki. Yes, he must ask Perk to help too in the Sunday school, perhaps even in the weeknight meeting he meant soon to institute and in the cottage meetings he had also planned. He must see Perk to-morrow and leave Taft till next day. He felt easier now that he had made up his mind to try what personal influence would do. He looked out again. The glow was dimmer in the northern sky. He glanced across at Taft. The thick mistbank had gathered down behind the house, which stood out dark against it, and seemed much bigger than it really was. He saw the small, black window on the gable, and stood looking at it till it vanished in the fog. He did not know that this time was the first of many times. Then he went to bed and lay awake a long while thinking over all his plans. That night he dreamed that Inga came close to him and her deep blue eyes looked into his, then she blushed and bent her head and her face was hidden by the red rim of her hat round which a fly was hurrying; but he saw her mouth and chin in the shade beneath the rim and they remained in sight. Next day, this dream and the thought of Inga as she looked when they first met came often to his mind and bothered him.

Between five and six o'clock next afternoon he walked up along the strip of heather damp with mist and knocked at the door of the Schoolhouse. Hakki himself opened it.

"Hallo, it's you, is it? Come along in," he said abruptly, after swallowing a little bit of bread and butter he was chewing. He had a small book in his hand. His short red hair was standing straight up on his head, and, now his hat was off, his left eye seemed to be more bent than ever on discovering what the right one was about. This squint was so pronounced that it held Mr. Mann's attention for a moment, for Perk's abruptness had disturbed his usual calmness and carefulness of manner. He was about to say, "Good evening," when Hakki broke out with,

"Well, what are you standing staring at? Are you thinking that St. Lucy must have had a holiday when I was born? Come in, man."

They entered a little parlour on the right, Mr. Mann feeling somewhat nervous over this unceremonious reception. Hakki pointed to a big armchair beside the fire.

"There you are," he said, "sit down. Will you have a cup of tea?" He stopped at the corner of a table in the middle of the room, where a small tray with tea things stood among a mass of books and papers, all of which, however, were arranged in order.

"No, thank you," said Mr. Mann, "I had tea just before coming up."

"All right," said Perk. "You smoke, don't you?"

"Yes."

"Well, light your pipe, while I finish stoking." He stood and slowly drank his second cup.

"You've a lot of literature here on the table," said Mr. Mann, lighting his pipe, and feeling he must be more free and easy than he usually was, "May I take a look at one or two of these small volumes?"

"Yes," answered Hakki, between two sips, "but lay them back exactly where you took them from." Mr. Mann had lifted one or two small science primers.

"These are some small prizes for the youngsters," said Hakki, finishing the tea and setting down the cup. He took his pipe from his writing-desk, where it had been lying, and sat down opposite to Mr. Mann.

"You shouldn't smoke within at least ten minutes after finishing a meal," said Mr. Mann.

"I know," replied Hakki, scratching a match.

"You don't need your prizes till September. How have you got them so soon?" asked Mr. Mann.

Hakki laughed and sent out a cloud of smoke.

"You are talking of the few, brief, religious treatises that their illiterate majesties, the members of the Board, will give as prizes in September; but that is not what I am thinking of at all," said he. He was in one of his sarcastic moods, which came upon him frequently when out of school, where he was never known to be sarcastic, and this one was bitterer than usual, for he had not yet got over Inga's conduct yesterday. Mr. Mann was nettled at this tone, as he himself had just been chosen by the members of the Board to fill the seat left vacant by the death of Mr. Wood; but he showed no sign, for he felt that he was in a parish where some tact would be required.

"How do you use these prizes then?" he asked, with a forced smile.

"I'll soon make that clear to the comprehension of even a layman," answered Hakki, sending out more smoke. "In the first place, the system usually adopted is utterly rotten. Do you see that?"

"You seem rather fond of making general assertions," said Mr. Mann, giving a quiet puff, "I can't say I exactly see it." Hakki looked at him across his nose and said with a short laugh,

"You think my view oblique. You can't forget St. Lucy's negligence. But I did not expect that you would see it, even though I use the method of instruction like yourself. I will prove the point; but what would become of you if you were asked to prove the general assertions you make from the pulpit? I know what you are going to say. You are going to quote Tennyson with his 'believing where we cannot prove,' but I won't have it. If you go 'believing where you cannot prove,' I will take the wiser course of 'proving where I cannot believe.'"

"My goodness, Mr. Perk," said Mr. Mann, his argumentative instincts rising in him, "is this not quite uncalled for?"

"You sit quite still and take your turn in the pew," said Hakki, giving a short laugh again, "I did not think that you would see the point. You are one of the engineers who work that old, soul-saving machine you call the Church. One can't expect you to see things at first. You're in the 'cast-your-deadly-doing-down' business. You put your rags in the slot and get a new garment out. You believe that the Eternal Spirit guts the repentant sinner like a herring, takes his old heart clean out of him and sticks a brand new heart in where the old one was."

Mr. Mann began to think that Perk would not be suitable for cottage meetings. He was troubled, but he smoked on quietly without interrupting him. He felt it much more difficult to speak in a rebuking tone to one of his own age and class than it had been to do so to old Magnus Sharp.

"Yes, that's about the size of your development," continued Hakki, with a sneer. "One really can't expect you to see anything in human effort. You're a smart engineer yourself, however. Mind you, I don't refuse to give you credit where I think you ought to have it."

"Thank you," said Mr. Mann, with a small touch of irony, "but what has this to do with the matter of the prizes?"

"You cannot see it yet," said Hakki, somewhat banteringly, "Well, look you here. I give a prize each quarter to every youngster who can beat himself or herself by a reasonable percentage; not who can beat his neighbour or her neighbour in a deadly strife of place taking. I do not set those small, totally depraved (?) beings against each other, but against themselves. I know by careful watching what each of them can do, and I expect accordingly. Every youngster in a class may win a prize by steady work. You see this small book I have in my hand. Well, it describes in very simple language how Man began to struggle slowly up from barbarism. Little Oli Jarmson will get it as his prize on Friday afternoon. He's not a brilliant boy by any means. If I allowed them to take places in the class, he would gravitate straight to the bottom; but he's an earnest, plodding little fellow, who thinks a good deal more than one who does not study children would believe. I give the younger children pictures, little prints of famous men, and things, and places in the world. The whole affair will cost me about fifteen shillings in the year. The few older ones that get the little books must bring them back each quarter, to let me see if they are taking care of them, then they may lend them to each other."

"What did you say that small book was about?" asked Mr. Mann in a rather serious voice. "Would you mind my looking at it for a moment?" He laid the ones he had been holding down upon his knee and took the other Hakki offered him. He turned over a few pages, then he looked across at Hakki.

"The main thing I had in mind in coming up," he said, "was to ask you to come and help me in the Sunday School." He thought, and with some slight annoyance, how differently this interview had gone from what he had anticipated. He had planned that he would lead the conversation, but that was not happening. Hakki laughed.

"Well, fire away," said he, "I've been talking shop the whole time myself. It's right enough that you should have a turn now."

"Will you come?" asked Mr. Mann, with a direct glance at him.

"No," answered Hakki, in a quieter tone than he had yet employed. "Your work is the Sunday; my work is the week. You are on quite other lines from me. You tell the youngsters in the Sunday School that Adam fell; if I were to come there to help you, I should have to tell them that he rose."

"What do you mean?" asked Mr. Mann, in a voice somewhat constrained, and feeling that next time he spoke he must say Sabbath School instead of Sunday School.

CHAPTER VI

AN IMPULSE

"Nihil fieri sine causa potest."—CICERO

"MEAN?" echoed Hakki. "Simply what I say. You would not care to know of such instruction being given in your church on Sunday, I imagine."

"The purpose of the Sabbath School," said Mr. Mann, a little coldly, "is to give such instruction to the children as shall tend to make them wise unto salvation. They have souls to save. It is the duty of their teachers to keep that in view above all else."

Perk gave a short, hard laugh.

"Perhaps it would not hurt their souls to hear a little plain truth now and then," he said.

Mr. Mann made a slight, nervous movement with the hand that held the book.

"You imply they do not hear it very often," said he, in a quiet, but firm tone. He looked at Hakki steadily.

"What do you think yourself?" asked Hakki bluntly. He blew a cloud of smoke halfway across the room.

"I must differ from you on that point," said Mr. Mann more firmly still.

"Thank you for letting me see these," he added. He handed back the little book he had been holding, and, rising, laid the others on the table in their proper place; then he sat down again.

"No doubt," returned Hakki, smiling. "You must defend your business. But we needn't quarrel over it. Your pipe is empty, man. Have a fill of this. It's Faithful Lover; very good tobacco, though you may feel it just a trifle strong at first. An old school chum keeps me supplied with it." He took a dark cake from the table-drawer and offered it to Mr. Mann.

"No, thanks," replied the minister, a little stiffly; "I prefer smoking duty-paid tobacco."

"O, very well," said Hakki, grinning; "Church and State, of course. I might have noticed. You have some of the orthodox narcotic there. Light up. Here's the matches. They're all right."

Hakki was irritated more than he would have cared to say, both at Inga's manner to him and to Bob, and at Mr. Mann for having made him feel more interest than he had meant to feel in each of the two sermons he had heard from him.

"Well, I suppose I need not offer you a glass of Faroe brandy," he went on.

"No, thanks," said Mr. Mann, filling his pipe with his cut cavendish and lighting it with one of the matches that had been certified "all right."

"Very good," said Hakki. "You're not in a hurry.

Old Kirsty Jeemson who keeps house for me is up at Hooll; but she'll be back between eight and nine and then we'll have a bite of supper."

"No, thank you," said the minister; "I will not stay to-night."

"Please yourself," returned Hakki, and then they both sat silent for a while.

From where Mann was sitting he could see right down the valley. Down at the foot of it, beside the shore, the Ha loomed white through the thin haze that veiled the landscape, and as his eyes fell on it he remembered he had heard that the laird's daughter was soon coming home from school. That was another he would try to get. She will surely take an interest in church work, he thought. He did not think that she might chance to take an interest in himself. Then he thought again of Inga, and his dream came and bothered him once more. He could not understand how such a trifling thing should keep on coming up before him in this way. His thoughts came round again to Hakki's words, and he felt a little saddened. But he determined that he would be cautious with Hakki till he knew him better. He saw that Hakki's energy and his strong sense of order would be very useful if he could but win them for the work he wished to further. But he was not very clear as to the way in which it would be best to bring the matter up again. He felt inclined to tell Perk very plainly what he thought of those strange views he had expressed; but he kept this feeling down, because he was afraid, not in the least of Hakki or his sarcasm, but of the effect his words might have in pushing them still farther from each other.

He rose from his chair and stood for a little on the hearthrug in front of the empty fireplace, looking at the few articles that were arranged upon the narrow mantel-shelf. Hakki was closely watching him.

A framed photograph of Inga was standing there, just in the shadow of a small, metal timepiece, which kept ticking vigorously. He did not notice it at first, for his attention had been caught by a minute pair of Dutch clogs and a minute pair of sealskin slippers of Esquimaux work, which stood together on a small model of a "bass" or straw doormat. Then, all at once, he saw Inga looking at him from the shadow. The look was so lifelike that it sent over him the same, strange feeling he had had when first their eyes had met. His dream, too, rose up in his mind again. It was so unexpected that it startled him a little, and a faint blush came to his face. He wondered whether Hakki had observed this, and he began to speak to him in a somewhat hesitating way about the tiny slippers and the clogs upon the mantelpiece. A few minutes afterwards he turned round and said,

"I will be going now."

"You have not stayed long," said Hakki, with a smile. "I will come up some other evening and stay longer," returned Mr. Mann, glancing quickly at him.

"That's right," said Hakki, rising, "You run alongside of me for a bit, till we see if we can suit each other. If we can't, then you up-helm and bear away."

He went with Mr. Mann to the door, where they shook hands.

Hakki stood and watched the minister's black hat, pale face, and black shoulder pass along the top of the low, whitewashed wall, that bounded the small schoolhouse garden, then his long, black back and legs move slowly off along the slope and down towards the Manse.

"That little, blue-eyed witch has looked at him, I guess, and he has felt it," he muttered to himself as he turned back into the parlour. He went straight to the mantelpiece and looked at Inga's photograph.

"You little monkey," he said, pointing at it with the stem of his pipe. Then he sat down and thought of Inga. He knew she did not care a bit for Bob, and that was why he felt so angry at her, for he had seen her plainly acting to Bob yesterday as if she did. He had never seen her acting so before, and he said to himself that it was mean and almost heartless for he was quite sure that Bob was nearly desperate about her. He had, himself, a feeling for her somewhat warmer than the merely cousinly. He was quite aware of that and so was Inga. It would not, however, have been very painful to him, had she really cared for Bob, for he felt that Bob would well deserve some real affection in return for the great love he gave. But he felt his pulses quicken at the thought that Mr. Mann might somehow come into the matter. His irritation over Inga's altered manner towards Bob, for which he could not yet account, began now to give way a little before this new but gradually growing apprehension.

When Mr. Mann reached home he found his mother in the dining-room.

“Mr. Bolt has been here asking us to come to Taft and have tea with them to-morrow afternoon,” she said.

“O yes,” he said, a little absently, for he was thinking about Hakki; “I was intending to call there to-morrow in any case. What did you say?”

“I told him we would come,” said Mrs. Mann.

“Quite so,” he said, and, walking to a window, stood there looking out upon the voe. The haze was clearing off and the evening sunshine had begun to flood the brown hills of the other shore.

After supper, he strolled down towards Da Point, still thinking about Hakki. When he reached the churchyard, he leaned against the east dyke for a while and looked in meditatively at the low graves, all overgrown with the rank grass and nettles, above which the very few headstones rose sadly up as if to show how very few of those that pass away are kept in memory by those they leave behind. The dark side of the gravestones was towards him, for the sun was in the west-north-west. This seemed to him a symbol of the dead that lay beneath and of the mystery of death itself; for the blackness was towards the mortal eye and the brightness on the other side.

"Yes; for each child of God," he murmured to himself. He thought of the hard lives that most of them had led; of their toils and dangers on the sea; how after all their storms and shipwrecks God had brought them back to rest here in this quiet haven on their native shore; while fathers, brothers, sons, of those that slumbered here, lay in strange lands and oceans far away. Some of the sleepers resting there had never been from home; but to them, too, the agony and peril of the sea had come. He thought of the sore sorrows that the hearts, now lying stilled beside him, once had borne; of the black-edged letter that had come and swept away all comfort from the hearts of aged parents, all gladness from a sister's face, and all the light and joy from the fond heart of her who waited hoping that the loved one would return.

"What would life mean if earth and time were all?" he murmured to himself. Yes; in the midst of all the sadness that tinged dark the life about him, his theme had been Praise, praise to Almighty God for that strong faith that triumphs over death and human woe.

"Praise be to God who giveth us the victory," he said more loudly, "through His own Son, our Lord and Saviour, Jesus Christ." Was anything on earth to be compared with this, even for a single moment? What human science or philosophy could give to these poor, bleeding hearts the consolation Christ could give?

He moved on slowly in the narrow path that ran along below the churchyard wall, on out along the banks and round Da Point. He almost shuddered now as he remembered some of Hakki's words and the tone in which they had been uttered. When he got to Da Point he went down the banks to where the black rocks formed a kind of chamber with its opening towards the voe. He sat down on a small ledge at the back, and looked out over the still voe with its calm surface touched by the last brightness of the sun, which Da Aest Hill was just about to hide.

"I wonder how Perk treats the Bible in the school?" he said aloud. "I must enquire regarding that." He felt a hot flush pass over him, at the thought that he had not denounced Perk's views upon the spot; but he felt glad next moment that he had not done so and that he still might have a chance of influence with him. Yes; he would give his people more than ever the plain, the grand, old Gospel, and rouse them into burning zeal for God. The picture of the few that slept in church rose up before him. It chilled him. But he would go to them at home, as he had purposed. Then Inga's deep blue eyes looked into his. It was his dream again. No other eyes that he had seen had looked at him with so much sympathy. But that photograph on Hakki's mantelpiece! He wondered why such things would come and push themselves into the midst of earnest thoughts.

The rocky chamber in which he was sitting was just beside the cove in which the herring-boat had lain. A bare, grisled head was looking carefully in over the edge of the big, flat rock that formed its north wall, and down at Mr. Mann. If Mr. Mann had not been looking at the sea, he would have seen the shadow of the head on the rockwall to the right.

"Inga boanie lass," said a voice right above him. Mr. Mann jumped up, and, standing on the ledge, looked over the flat rock. He saw Jacob shuffling off along the white sand of the cove as fast as he was able.

The tea at Taft had been a little plan of Inga's. That morning she had risen restless and dissatisfied for the first time in her life. She could not get rid of the thought that she had acted meanly towards Bob. Sometimes she wished she had not spoken to him so at the kirk door and brought him back, that she had left him quite alone to stop away if he wished to do so. Then her mood would change and vanity would tell her once more that she could not have endured to see him go and to have Janny and the other girls laughing at her. This mood came oftener than the other all through the forenoon and up till dinner-time. She thought a good deal also about Mr. Mann. Her wish that he might come to Taft that day grew stronger. It was strengthened by her restlessness. Two or three times, on going from the shop into the house, she went out round the south end of the house and entered by the kitchen door, and each time she did this she glanced towards the Manse. Late in the afternoon she saw his head above the strip of heather as he went up in the direction of the Schoolhouse. Then it flashed upon her mind that it would be a good idea to ask him and Mrs. Mann to tea next afternoon, and she at once spoke to her mother about this. Willa was quite eager for it, but when Inga wanted her to put on her new bonnet and go over to the Manse to give the invitation, she drew back at once, for she knew well enough how such a thing would look.

"Na, lass," she said, "da laek o dat wid onnly mak a spaekalation among da folk." So it was settled to send Hansi, and after Inga had brushed and scrubbed him for a while and made him put on his next best coat and hat, which he wore always when he went to pay his rent, he was allowed to go.

"Mistress Mann is a rael fine body," he said heartily when he came back. "Shö said dey wid be blyde ta come."

When Mr. and Mrs. Mann came to Taft next afternoon Inga met them at the door. She had pushed unpleasant thoughts quite from her for the present. Her manner was all heartiness and kindness mixed with a certain shy respectfulness that captivated Mrs. Mann. Willa sat on the bulky haircloth sofa with her volume of the "Christian Treasury" beside her, as if she had just laid it down. The formal visit of a minister had always to her mind something of the Sabbatic about it. Mr. Mann half expected to see Hakki in the parlour when he entered, but Hakki was not there. Willa had as an afterthought wished to ask him, but Inga and Hansi had overruled her. She had wished to have Hakki so that she might have what she deemed a learned young man of her own, as it were, to play off against Mrs. Mann's learned young man; but Inga and Hansi objected, each for a different reason. When Mrs. Mann came downstairs again from the best bedroom whither she had been taken by Inga, Willa, having welcomed her in an effusive manner, began at once about her book, as the best substitute for Hakki's learning she could think of, praised it highly, and even offered to lend it to Mrs. Mann.

Mr. Mann could see that Inga was annoyed at Willa's volubility, and that Willa disregarded several winks and hints that Inga gave her. Mrs. Mann seemed so completely interested that Willa fully thought that Inga was quite silly in her efforts to repress her. Hansi had to mind the shop, and that left Inga to look after Mr. Mann.

When tea was over, Mrs. Mann and Willa got on the sofa together and opened the personal narrative vein, a thing they were both anxious to do. Mrs. Mann had certainly felt lonely since she came to Norwik, for she had not grown intimate with Mrs. Black, whom she did not like and who was sometimes not in a fit state to receive her when she called.

"Yes, I feel it rather dull at times," she said in her low, gentle voice. "My son is so taken up with his books and studies. Sometimes I think he should not read so much, for with his abilities he could preach quite well with far less reading. He has known the saving power of the blood of Christ, and his heart is burning with zeal for the good of souls."

"Yis, yis," said Willa, "dat's da wirds o truth. We never hed da laek o him here afore."

"Poor lad," continued Mrs. Mann softly, in a tone that could not carry to where Mr. Mann and Inga sat, looking over an old album Inga had produced, "I hope there are not many who must go through his experience. I shall never forget your husband's friendliness in the old, dark days." Willa gave an elongated sigh.

"Yea, Hansi haes a kind hert," she said, "bit it wis nothin bit his duty. Shörly, shörly, he wis met wi kindness dere afore." Mrs. Mann bent nearer and tears were in her eyes.

"That awful night," she said, "when I was forced to take the infant in my arms and fly from my own house because his father in his drunken rage was threatening to kill both him and me and then himself, your husband, who was in the town, went in and stayed with him all night, and was the means in God's hands, I believe, of saving him from self-destruction. Yes, poor lad, what a childhood! Even after his father had been converted and had turned to hate the drink, the temper was no better. He grew so strict and terrible towards the boy, and thrashed him often cruelly for little bits of disobedience that were almost nothing, and all my pleading could not save him. Many a night the poor little fellow after such a thrashing crept from his own bed and across the stairhead to Naanie Smith, our servant, for he dared not come to me for comfort, and Naanie had to take him in beside her and let him sob himself to sleep in her kind arms. I don't know how I could have borne it all if I had not had Naanie. I was almost thankful, God forgive me, when the illness came that struck my husband down and the doctor told me that there was no hope."

The rich evening glow fell softly into the corner of the room where Mr. Mann and Inga sat. Their chairs were close together by a small, square table on which the album lay, and sometimes Mr. Mann's left knee touched Inga's right. This time Inga used a haircloth chair and not the one that Bob had made. In the soft, warm light her smiling face was prettier than ever. Each time Mr. Mann asked her about a photograph he raised his eyes and looked at her, and each time that he looked a thrill shot through him. One time he was startled as he felt a powerful impulse move him to suddenly bend nearer and press a kiss upon her rosy mouth. He was so startled that he felt he must compel himself to serious thoughts, and he said quickly,

"I am anxious to get one or two good teachers for the Sabbath School. Will you come, Miss Bolt, and help me?" Inga's heart jumped. The "Miss Bolt" fell sweetly on her ears. She could not help contrasting its politeness with Bob's plain, "Inga, lass."

"Yes," she said, looking at him with a grateful glance, "I will be very glad to come." He scarcely knew himself whether he was glad or not; there was something so disturbing in these new sensations he felt growing in him.

"Thank you," he said quietly; but he was thinking of that photograph on Hakki's mantelpiece.

Three hours later, when he and Mrs. Mann were walking slowly back towards the Manse, his mother said to him,

"Mr. Bolt's daughter is really a very pretty girl, and warm-hearted. There is a certain refinement about her too. I do not wonder that, as Mrs. Bolt was telling me, Jeems Ertirson's son Bob is almost desperate about her."

"O yes," he answered with a slight flush which his mother did not notice.

CHAPTER VII

VATSTER

"On n'apprend pas aux hommes à être honnêtes gens."—PASCAL

"GOOD morning," said Mr. Mann, bending his head as he went in at the low door of Vatster in response to a loud "Come in," from the interior, that had followed instantly upon his knock.

"Good mornin, sir," answered Aald Erti jerkily, as he jumped up from the resting-chair, where he had been sitting sorting a small fishing-line, and came to the door of the "but-end." He started up as if he had known nothing till that moment of Mr. Mann's approach; but he had been told of it by Janny, who had seen Mr. Mann as soon as he came round below the School and turned north for Vatster, and who stood now in undress uniform in a corner hidden from the door and signalled violently to her father to take the minister at once into the "ben" room. Aald Erti had begun to sort the line in a great hurry, because, for reasons of his own, he wished the minister to find him busy when he entered.

"This way, sir; ye'll grant me pardon, sir, for goin before my betters, sir," he said, pushing open the crazy "ben" door, and Mr. Mann stepped in upon the creaking wooden floor. Aald Erti had been one of the seven sleepers, although he had been only three times at the kirk since Mr. Mann's induction. He pulled Mr. Mann by the arm to a chair, which he dusted with the flat of his hand, and seizing the minister's hat and stick, laid them on a little teakwood table that needed dusting much more than the chair, in Mr. Mann's opinion.

"This is very speecial wedder, sir," he said, taking a chair himself, and glancing sideways at the minister with his sly gray eyes.

"Yes; it is remarkably fine weather," said Mr. Mann.

"Yes, sir," said Aald Erti, "as you say, sir, he's remarkable fine wedder, sir, and very necessitous."

"You mean necessary," said Mr. Mann in a kindly tone. "Yes; we have great cause to thank God for His goodness to us in this respect."

"Yes, sir; as you say, sir," said Aald Erti glibly, "them's the very wirds, now, I made use of, sir, last Sunday at the kirk door. I said, says I, 'Yes men,' says I, 'this is relly very necessitous wedder both for the fishin and so for the crops, and we hev great cause to thenk God for His goodness to us all.' Them was my wirds, yes; it was just before you goed in, sir, and owld John Jarmson was standing there, sir, and my son Erti, and the boys, and they'll tell you the very same. Yes, I said to them all, sir, the same as I'm sayin it to you just now; I says, says I, 'This is rel—'"

"Quite so," said Mr. Mann, gently but firmly.

"I ask your pardon, sir," said Erti, stopping.

"I said, 'Quite so,'" returned Mr. Mann.

"Yes, certainly, sir," said Erti. "Well, as I was sayin, sir, I'm a little dull, for the most part, in my hearin now. I've not lived here all my time, no; I've had to knock about the world, sir. I've had to wrastle with it, and a man's frame can't last for ever; some of your fixins is bound to give way, sir."

"You have not lived always in Norwik, then?" said Mr. Mann.

"No, sir," returned Erti, "I was sailin all the first of my time, and I was in Canady for five year."

"O, yes," said Mr. Mann.

"Yes," continued Erti, the floodtide of his reminiscences beginning to come in, "it's no wonder that my hearin is a little dull, sir, after the cowld I had to siffer there. You've been in Canady, sir?"

"No," said Mr. Mann, waving aside the compliment.

"Well, sir," said Erti, feeling safer in free treatment of his subject, "I tell you it ain't no joke, and the cowld out there comes on so suddent like. I seen the ducks swimmin in the river, sir, on a fine, beautiful mornin as ever comed out of the sky, and in ten seconds they was all froze up, and we had to hokk (dig) them out with our hatchets, sir, when we comed hom at dinner-time."

"Dear me," said Mr. Mann, dubiously. Then he asked, "What were you doing in Canada?"

"Doin, sir?" said Erti, with a touch of his dignified manner, "I was persecutin my calling, sir." Mr. Mann could hardly repress a smile.

"You were prosecuting your calling," said he; "what calling, may I ask?"

"Well, sir," answered Erti, "it was ston-work for the most part; but I did somethin in wood-work too, sir, in a menner of speakin. I was alwas a handy man, and could turn my ten fingers to anything."

"Are you a native of this parish?" asked Mr. Mann.

"O yes," said Erti, importantly. "My father had his origin in Nestin; but I myself was born, for the most part, in Norwik." This time Mr. Mann could not repress his smile. He turned his face away, and the left corner of his mouth went nearly to his ear; but Erti did not see this. He felt that he must laugh when he got by himself.

"I am hoping to see you oftener at church," he said, slowly turning his head again.

"Yes, sir, and that's what you will," returned Erti, folding his arms and sitting straight up in his chair like a man who was quite clear about his duty and meant to do it thoroughly. "The discoorses you give us is not a thing to pass, sir. Mester Wood, the owld minister, was a good man, in a menner of speakin, and a well-learned man; but he didn't preach the Blod, sir. You never got a rael Gospel discoorse from him. I don't want to judge my neebour, sir; but I can't say that he was a convertit man. He would lin his elbik on the book-board there, and give us a sort of a kind of a yarn about the owld prophets and suchlike away in the forepart of the Scripter; but that couldn't save your sowl, sir. Now, there was the sermon you gave us last Sunday, about Prayer and waitin upon God, sir. I say that was the rael, genuine Gospel, and no mistake about it."

Mr. Mann gave a slight cough.

"About the Praise waiting for God," he said quietly, with an emphasis on the first noun.

"Exactly so, sir," said Erti, unfolding his arms and bringing his hands smartly down on his knees, "that's what I say, the 'Praise waitin for God.' It was a powerfil edifeein discoorse. I havn't heard the like of it in ten year."

Erti had managed to catch the text imperfectly before going off into his doze, a thing he usually remedied by getting it the right way from Janny or Young Erti when they all came home. This time he had neglected to do so, for he had not thought that he would need it quite so soon. Mr. Mann fixed him with his eye.

"I did not think you were listening," he said, in a slightly louder tone. "It seemed to me that you were sleeping."

Erti sat up in his chair again, and gave a forgiving little laugh.

"That I can well believe, sir," he said, eagerly, his sly gray eyes alternately meeting and avoiding the minister's. "It's a kind of a way I have, and a kind of a way I've had all my time, and my father afore me, sir. As soon as you gives out the text, I shuts my eyes; and I hears the whole sermon twize as good that way. Yes, upon my s-so—! sir; beg pardon, sir. Yes, I treasures every wird."

"You find it an aid to introspection," said Mr. Mann smoothly.

"Ta be sure, sir," responded Erti, emphatically, bringing his hands again down on his knees.

"Mr. Wood was a good man, I believe," said the minister.

"Well, yes, sir; in a menner of speakin he was," returned Erti, cautiously. "Him and me didn't get on so well as we soud have don but for some of my fine neebours. I used to look after the glibe for him, and, as you sees yourself, sir, it lies quite disjacent to the fut of my own croft; my mödow and the glibe mödow is both alongside of the burn there. Well, it was no disconvennience to me to see after the place for the owld gentleman, and wan day he comes here to Vatster and he says, 'Arthur' says he, 'I wants to speak with you about somethin,' says he; and—"

"And he wished you to manage the glebe for him," said Mr. Mann, anxious to cut short the circumstantial narrative, which he saw was about to follow.

"Just exackly, sir," said Erti promptly, lifting his hands and bringing them down with a smack upon his knees again, "and if it hadn't hev been as a obleedgement to the owld gentleman and him bein my minister, in a menner of speakin, I soud never have had nothin to do with it, sir, for its a nasty lump of ground and as hard as h-h-horn, sir. Yes, it is that in f-f-f-fack, sir; nothin but slavery of a man's life to laabour it up."

"Mr. Wood asked you, then, as a great favour to undertake the work?" suggested Mr. Mann.

"Well, sir," said Erti, carefully, "I woon't deny that I did just mention the metter to him wan day afore; but that was out of kinsideration for hisself, sir, because I seen he was put about." He would not risk sailing too far from the coast of truth.

"Mr. Wood had evidently wished to relieve you of so distressing a charge," said Mr. Mann.

"I found Oli Jarmson weighted with it when I came."

"I don't want to judge my neebour, sir;" said Erti, leaning towards the minister and almost whispering, "but I tell you this out of respeck, sir, and hopes you woon't lay my name to it, sir, that you better keep an eye on Oli, for there's certain peckings about a glibe, sir, as you knows, and excep a man's honest like myself as would rather femish as take the wirth of a bled of grass that belonged another, he comes to be, in a menner of speakin, in temptation; yes, and the Scripter says, as you knows better as I can tell you, 'Laed us not into temptations, but deliver us from evil,' which is sound doctrin, sir, and no mistake."

"Do you mean to say that Oli Jarmson is not honest?" asked Mr. Mann significantly.

"Me, sir? God forgive you,—beg pardon, sir,"—said Erti, quickly, fearing he had gone too far. "No, no; Oli is as true as steel. There's not a honester man in all Shetland. It's not that sir. It's his experrience. He has no experrience. The man is young, and you can't expeck it of him, and then he's lived up there in Da Krö all his time with non to taech him anything, excep that owld father of his that's goin now twofald with rheumatics and ain't been out in the world to learn nothin hisself, sir. No, no; I says nothin again' the men; but ye'll have a cup of tea, sir."

Before Mr. Mann had time to utter a word he was up and off into the other room, where Janny was sitting speculating on the most suitable form of refreshment. He closed both doors after him.

"Haes du any tay ready, lass?" he asked as he closed the "but" one.

"Is du offered him a gless o speerits?" asked Janny in a hoarse whisper that almost penetrated through both doors to Mr. Mann.

"No, I foryat," returned Erti jerkily. He had been too anxious to get out of the room and so create a diversion before bringing up the glebe again, that he had clean forgotten to suggest the spirits.

"O daa, du is a föl," snapped Janny, looking Aald Erti dead in the eye. "Didna I tell dee ta offer him da speerits first? Du didna go an spaek till him aboot tay first, did du?"

"Howld dy tongue," retorted Erti. "He said that he wid laek a cup of tay. See if du can make it ready, without any more lip about it."

"It's staandin here ready ta lift ben," said Janny, saving up her repartee till after the departure of the minister.

"All right," cried Erti, "come ben at wance efter me." He seized the small fishing line still lying on the resting-chair, and went "ben" again, leaving both doors open.

"Ye'll excuse me, sir, for takin this in my hand; but I can't bear to be idle, sir. Janny is just comin with a cup of tea, sir. You'll take a dish of tea. It's not much to offer you for the most part; but it's from the hert, as you knows, sir."

"You needn't have troubled about that," said Mr. Mann.

"Trouble; it's no trouble to the likes of Janny, sir," said Erti, with what was meant for an indulgent, fatherly smile towards his bulky daughter, who was entering with a small, weatherbeaten tray with two cups on it in her hands. Janny had hurried on her Sunday dress over her weekday one, the draggled edge of which showed out below the other, and she had cursorily washed her "janteel" face, leaving what youngsters call a "flöd-mark" to indicate that it was a case of saying to the water, "Hitherto shalt thou come and no further." After she and Mr. Mann had greeted each other, Erti continued,

"Ever since her that belonged to me was taken, sir, now eight year back last Candlesmas, she's keepit the house goin for me and Erti the same as her mother was wint to do. Ay, that was a clever wumman, sir, never idle a moment, and alwas keepin everything like the preen." He gave an exaggerated sigh, while Mr. Mann sat thinking that, if Janny's mother had so strong an antipathy to dust, Janny had somehow managed to avoid inheriting it.

"Mebbe ye wid hev pirferred a gless of speerits, sir," said Janny apologetically.

"No, thank you, Janet; this is much better," answered Mr. Mann, feeling, however, his conscience slightly troubling him as he observed the strength of the decoction Janny was now pouring out.

"Ye'll ask a blissin, sir," said Erti, his tone betraying the great rarity of such a thing at other times.

"Du'll tak a cup with da minister, faeder," said Janny, when this was done; then she sat down to listen to the conversation.

"Well, sir," went on Erti, putting his knees close together and setting the cup and saucer on them, but still keeping the line in his lap as if this tea-drinking was merely an interlude, "as I was sayin, her that belonged to me, yes; that was the clever wumman and no mistake. She fell badly about Hallowmas, and it took her with a particlar faerce cough, sir, and she takes to her bed. After a time we fetches the doctor, and he comes back and fore, and back and fore, and then wan day he takes me ben here, by ourselves like, and he sets him down on the very same shair that you're sittin on now, sir, and he says, says he, 'Arthur, this is a bad business,' says he. 'Sir,' says I, 'What is it that she's got now?' says I. 'It's brownkeeties,' says he, with a kind of a gron, sir. 'My Go-g-goodness!' says I,—Beg pardon, sir,—with a face as white as that fine, white shirt you've got on now, sir, and he seen I was going to swound, and so he jumps up and gives me a bong in the back and a gless of speerits, which is handy to have in the house, sir, in a time of illness; and at Candlesmas she wears awey, and we is all left prostitute with sifferin, sir."

He took a big, consoling sip of tea and smacked his lips.

Mr. Mann thought the moment favourable for bringing up the week-night meeting.

"Yes, it must have been a very painful period for you," he said quietly. "At such a time the heart feels its great need of consolation, and there is only one Physician."

"Well, yes, sir," said Erti. "I thought myself at the time that it would have been better to have a consolation as you says, and I seen the thing don often out in Whebec. They does it with two doctors, sir; but, as you says, we had onnly the wan doctor here, excep we'd gone and fetched wan from Lerrick."

"I referred to the consolation of religion," said Mr. Mann, wishing to humour him round.

"Exackly so, sir," responded Erti, heartily, as if his soul had invariably been filled with it. "Nothin can beat it, sir. Mester Wood, he seen as how we was lyin prostitute with sifferin, and he comed and prayed off and on like and lifted us up, and it was just about that time that he gave me the glibe to look after; and if you yourself, sir, wants a experrienced man to take charge of it for you, I'm willin, out of respeck to you, sir."

Mr Mann did not like being turned aside again.

"I thought you told me that it was too much for you," he said, a little firmly.

"Not me, sir," returned Erti quickly, setting his cup back on the table and beginning to busy himself with his line. "Though it was hard work I'd have keepit it, sir, but for the lies that some of my fine neebours went and made on me."

"We need not speak further about that," said Mr. Mann. "I have no intention of making any change."

He turned his head and looked through the not particularly transparent window at the sunny landscape of the valley, and as he did so, Aald Erti and Janny exchanged a look.

"I am about to begin a weeknight prayer meeting," he said after a little, turning his head again and setting his cup on the table. "It will be commenced in the end of harvest, as it would be impossible to get many people to attend much sooner. Those living hereabout, of course, I hope to see attending regularly. Meanwhile, I intend to make more of the Sabbath school, and I hope you will make its success a matter of earnest prayer. I am trying to obtain fresh workers, and I expect to find sufficient interest existing to give me eager helpers in that honourable work. You will all be glad to see it prosper."

"Ta be sure, sir," said Erti, affecting a frank heartiness he was very far from feeling. "Its been a graet want in the place for long. The shildren oucht relly to be learned more about their Saviour, sir, and suchlike, for it says in the Scripter, 'Siffer little shildren to come unto Me,' yes, and them's His own wirds as you knows. Janny there will be glad to come and give you a hand, sir, with the Sunday school. She's a good lass, and reads her Bible reglar every Helly, sir; she does that, in f-f-fack, and she would be a graet help to you, being of a particlar turn with bairns, and she would be, for the most part, more as willin to come."

"That I wid indeed," said Janny promptly.

"Thank you, Janet," said Mr. Mann good-naturedly, "but Miss Bolt has already promised to come, and I am hoping to get Miss Black when she comes home, so in the meantime we shall have enough of lady teachers, if we could only get one or two more young men."

Mr. Mann thought of Hakki's words and felt that there was not a very great chance of being able to get him.

Janny gave an audible sniff; but Mr. Mann did not observe the angry look upon her face.

"Well, there's Erti, sir," said Aald Erti eagerly. "Yes, though I says it myself as is his father, in a menner of speakin, and mebbe shouldn't, he's the cleverest young fallow in the whole place, sir, excep perhaps the like of Perk there, down in the Schoolhouse. Erti would come in a moment, sir."

Just then a small, white pig, that had been arguing with a black hen outside the door as to the nature of the feast going on within, pushed up the crazy door with its snout and ran grunting expectantly into the room. The hen came hurrying behind it.

Janny sprang up and hustled the intruders out, in spite of all their protestations of previous intimacy with her. At the outer door she gave the little pig a kick that showed how strong her interest was in the fresh aspect of the Sunday school; but the little pig did not mind this very much, for Janny had only an old slipper on, which flew off, and which the small quadruped at once pursued and began to worry, while the hen ran scolding round the corner of the house.

As Janny came in again, having rescued her slipper, Mr. Mann rose to go.

"Well, I hope you will try to hold up my hands with prayer," he said, taking his hat and stick from the table, "so that I may feel that I have the full sympathy of my people in every endeavour to quicken and deepen the spiritual life here."

"Yes, sir; you can depend upon that, sir," said Aald Erti promptly, jumping up and proceeding ostentatiously to brush the dust from the back part of the minister's coat in flat defiance of his own expressed views as to Janny's tidiness. Janny shook hands with Mr. Mann without committing herself in any way to the holding up of hands. She had begun to feel that she would rather try to pull them down.

"Yes, sir," repeated Aald Erti, "you can that in f-f-fack, sir,—beg pardon, sir,—and if anything should happen about the glibe, sir, you knows as how I'd be more as willin to look after it for you at any moment, sir, and hopes you'll bear that in mind, sir."

Mr. Mann walked slowly off between the "rigs," while the small white pig stood looking after him as though it had not quite decided whether the left foot of his black trousers might not be much more interesting than Janny's slipper as a thing to worry.

Then Erti turned to Janny. They had both gone "but," and were standing looking out through the translucent window.

"Ay, ay," said he, with a malicious gleam in his eyes; "and yon's owld, drukken Mann's bit of white-faced boy that used to mizzur me out a gill of whisky when I was in the town with sheep. He dont let on about the like of that now. No, not he, feth. He's got an air with him now. We was all good enough then, as long as we had a red cent; but the likes of us is dirt now. Yes, feth, let him keep his damned owld glibe; but, by my sowl, I'm not don with Oli Jarmson yet."

"Yea, an heard du yon aboot Hansi's red gimmer?" said Janny, her eyes reflecting the malicious gleam in the old man's. "Da laek o it is ta be Miss Bult nu, an it's ta be a lady-taecher i da Sundy sköl. O, mi country! Dey wir shörly pride an stink anoff dere afore; bit wait dee, my lass, wait dee!"

CHAPTER VIII

DA HA

"Per occulta virtù."—DANTE

MRS. Black sat in her dining-room with Mary, who had just come home the day before. A small, black marble clock upon the mantelpiece had struck three with a sweet, silvery tinkle, and was now silently upon its way to four and to eternity. Mr. Black was in his office, as he called it, though Mrs. Black invariably spoke about it as the study. He usually took a nap there after dinner, which he had at two because he liked old ways.

"Have you seen much of the Manns, mamma?" asked Mary in a quiet voice, and with a comprehensive glance towards her mother, who leaned back in a semi-somnolent condition in her chair; but who at once blinked several times and pulled herself a little up.

"O yes, a good deal," she answered in a rather querulous tone that was habitual to her; "but not much just lately. They called last week, but I was too ill to see them."

Mary sighed. She knew quite well the nature of the illness.

"I am quite delighted with Mr. Mann," continued Mrs. Black, pulling herself up still more, while a gleam of something like enthusiasm passed over her dissatisfied face. "He is so eloquent, and he really knows how to behave. He has none of the awkwardness of manner you would have expected, knowing that his boyhood was spent in his father's shop."

"What is he like?" asked Mary. "I don't think I ever saw him."

"He's tall and dark," said Mrs. Black, "rather pale, with a small moustache, and he has big, dark eyes. He is really very good looking. Pa says that he is one of the ablest preachers for a young man he has ever heard; the only thing he would like different is that he was not quite so old-fashioned in his views; but I'm sure his views are right enough for the congregation he has to preach to, and quite according to the Bible and the Catechism. I don't understand why your pa should speak like that, for he doesn't at all like the new views that the people's minds are getting full of, about politics and land and everything, and I think it such a pity that things can't be left alone to go on as before; these new views and views are only making the people more and more discontented, and making them insolent too. Your pa should have more sense, and he is fond of old ways too, and won't on any account have dinner at a reasonable hour. I can't understand him."

"Pa reads a great deal," said Mary quietly, in a tone that showed that she for long had not deferred much to her mother's judgment upon anything, and that her sympathies were with her father to a great extent.

"Reads?" echoed Mrs. Black, her voice showing that she was not pleased at losing her usual after-dinner snooze. "I read as much and more myself, but I do not run off after all those silly notions. You are always defending your pa, Mary. You have always been fonder of him than of me."

Mary glanced at the heap of yellow-backs and fashion journals that covered a small table in the corner by her mother's chair, and smiled.

"Pa thinks a great deal too," she said.

"O yes," retorted Mrs. Black, "and I suppose I don't. They have not taught you delicacy in that school whatever else they have taught you, when you can speak so very sarcastically to me, the second day that you are home. But never mind, my dear. I have thought and thought till

I have grown quite stupid with it, and it has always been for you and pa, and now that you are grown up I will have to think still more, without even the small comfort of knowing that you believe I'm doing it."

Mrs. Black moved her right foot restlessly on the top of a very big, red rose, with which the hassock on which her flat foot was placed was ornamented. This rose seemed the keynote of Mrs. Black's ideas in regard to household decoration. Every surface that seemed able to take on a huge and gaudy flower had got one worked upon it. These tender blossoms looked as if they were meant to suggest the flora of a Paradise through which the mammoth and his inelegant contemporaries must have roamed, and that the nose of Father Adam must have been an object of some size in order to accommodate their fragrance. The room pained Mary's eyes, but she had not yet begun the ruin she intended.

"When old Mr. Mann died," continued Mrs. Black, proving her persistent thoughtfulness for her daughter by taking up the subject of the minister again, "he left a good deal of money; I don't know how much, but some thousands I believe. Mrs. Mann told me herself that she was very well left."

"There's the gate," said Mary suddenly, and turning her head she glanced through the window near which she was sitting, and saw Mr. and Mrs. Mann entering the garden. From what she had heard she knew them both at once.

They were shown into the dining-room. After the first greetings, Mrs. Mann sat down by Mrs. Black, while Mr. Mann took a low chair standing in the window near that of the young lady whom he knew now as Miss Black.

"You have just come home from Edinburgh?" he said, looking at her, and feeling himself to his annoyance, mentally contrasting her rather pale complexion with the bright face of Inga.

"Yes, from school there," she answered quietly.

"I passed some very happy years there myself, both at school and at college," he said slowly. "Previous to that my life had been in some ways rather hard. Do you like Edinburgh?"

"Yes, very much," replied Miss Black; "but it is pleasant to be home again, though there are always duties to face and some of them not of the most agreeable order."

She had a good deal of her father's outspokenness and his critical cast of mind.

Mr. Mann noticed this, and he could not help following out his silly fancy, as he thought it, of comparing her with Inga. She was taller than Inga, and her manner was more womanly, but her figure was much more girlish than that of Inga, whose girlishness was chiefly in her manner. Her eyes were hazel, and full of a soft light that seemed to indicate an element of dreaminess and fancy in her. Her hair was brown and wavy. She had a pretty nose, and a very pretty mouth and chin. There was a slight but distinct firmness about the mouth and chin, that made the face look purposeful and hinted at considerable strength of character. It seemed to Mr. Mann a face that could be proud, and patient too if there was need. There was no shadow of the dissatisfaction that the mother's face expressed. The girl's expression was one of kindly seriousness, shot through with the buoyancy of youth. It struck Mr. Mann so forcibly that it at once brought to his mind his own interest in her coming home, and he said presently,

"I am glad you have come home."

She looked at him frankly and gave a little smile. "Are you?" said she.

"Yes, I am glad," he said, and he could not help noticing the sweetness of her smile, "because I have been waiting to ask a favour of you."

He was conscious that the ministerial feeling he had had when he came in was changing to a feeling of companionship, though he could hardly understand why this was so.

"Will it be difficult to grant?" she asked, with the smile still on her lips.

"I do not think so," he said, with an answering smile. "It is that you will come and help me in the Sabbath School."

"That is very strange," she said brightly. "Before I left Edinburgh I had been planning to ask a favour of you, and it was that you would let me come and take a class on Sundays. I shall be delighted to do so. I have always thought that more should have been done in that way here."

"Thank you," said Mr. Mann. "It cheers me very much to find you sympathise so heartily and promptly with my effort. I have met with sympathy here certainly, but not in every quarter, and not at all in one case where I really counted on it."

"I think I know what you mean," she said. "You did not get it at the Schoolhouse. Mr. Perk holds such horrid views, and speaks so bluntly. I think he likes to shock people. He says such dreadful things. I have often wondered at papa for being so fond of him as he is. Papa goes up to him sometimes and occasionally has him down here. I told papa last summer when I was home that it was his duty as chairman of the Board to have him put away; but he only laughed and said he would not lose Perk for anything, for now he had someone worth talking to, and one who had put the rates down lower than ever they had been before."

"Yes, he is an excellent teacher, I believe," said Mr. Mann, "as far as school work is concerned; but my short interview with him left certainly rather a painful impression on my mind. The results of my four months ministry here have not at all been so encouraging as I had hoped."

He was surprised to find himself admitting this so freely to this girl whom he had never seen before. He did not care somehow to mention Inga's sympathy.

"I can easily understand that," she said. "You have set yourself so high an ideal that ordinary success looks just like failure."

He looked at her gratefully.

"I did not think of it in that way quite before," he said.

But he added almost instantly,

"I was not conscious of having an unusually high ideal. The ideal is in no way mine. I am simply one sent with a message, a Divine message, which should thrill every heart that hears it."

He did not think that this might be incipient scepticism. He was only thinking that this new sympathy was more intelligent if rather less warmhearted than the other.

"But," said Miss Black, "you have had great success already. Ma wrote to me that people had come from a distance, had been coming regularly to church since you were placed, people who never came near it before, and that some Sundays a great many had come across the voe in boats, a thing that Mr. Pirie will not much appreciate, I fear. Surely that indicates great interest in your work."

"Mary!" cried Mrs. Black from her armchair, where she had remained seated, discussing her favourite authors with Mrs. Mann who did not seem at all familiar with them. "What was the name of that book you brought home to me?"

Miss Black turned towards her mother.

"It was Dante," she answered.

"O yes, Dante's Divine Comedy," said Mrs. Black, promptly. "I read it long ago; but I don't like it nearly so well as his Faust."

Miss Black reddened a little.

"As his Faust, mamma?" she said "Don't you remember it was Goethe who wrote Faust?"

"O, of course," said Mrs. Black. "It's his Paradise Lost, I mean. It is so difficult to remember all these curious names."

"Yes, it is," said Mrs. Mann gently, feeling sorry for Miss Black, who took no notice of her mother's new departure.

Mr. Mann let the subject of the parish drop, and hurried to the rescue.

"Have you read much German, Miss Black?" he asked quickly.

Miss Black turned and looked at him.

"Yes," she answered eagerly, while Mrs. Black and Mrs. Mann proceeded with their conversation, "a good deal. I am very fond of it."

"I am very fond of it, also," he said, "but I have let my reading fall behind through want of time since I came here. Perhaps we might arrange to do a little reading now and then together."

"Yes, I should like that very much," returned Miss Black. "Pa and I read a lot last summer. I am sure that he would be delighted also. It will be so nice to have the three of us together."

A door banged in the back part of the house, and a little later, Mr. Black came into the dining-room. He shook hands with the visitors, and, walking to the fireplace, took a churchwarden from the rack beside the mantelpiece, and said,

"I think we'll all go into the garden and have tea there. Where's your pipe, Mr. Mann? The ladies don't mind our smoking. Come away."

They all rose and went into the garden, in the northeast corner of which was a little arbour of elder bushes perfumed by the delicate fragrance of the mignonette growing near. There were two long garden seats within, and Mrs. Black and Mrs. Mann sat down on one of them, while the two men took the other. Miss Black remained behind a little to tell Jeanie Ertirson to bring tea out to them in half an hour. As she came down the path past the tall hollyhocks which stood on either side, Mr. Mann saw how gracefully she moved. The afternoon sunshine fell in a flood through the opening of the bower, and struggled through the bushes.

"Well," said Mr. Black, lighting his churchwarden, "how are you getting on with your Sunday school extension scheme, Mr. Mann? You see we've got Mary there, home for all now. Have you been canvassing her?"

"Yes, I have," returned Mr. Mann, with a smile, "and she is greatly interested, and says that she will be delighted to assist me."

Miss Black sat down beside her father.

"You were telling me about a fortnight ago that you intended asking Perk to help you; did you do so?" asked Mr. Black, turning his thin, dark face and sharp eyes towards the minister. A faint touch of amusement was perceptible in his tone.

"I did," said Mr. Mann, a little nervously, taking his pipecase from his pocket, for Mr.

Black was fond of quizzing him, and he did not feel so nervous when he smoked.

"Well?" said Mr. Black, "and how did you get on? Perk is rather a strange fellow. Did he give you a wigging?"

"I did not at all like the tone of his remarks," answered Mr. Mann, hurriedly lighting his pipe.

For the moment he once more wished that he had contradicted Hakki, so that he could now have said that he had done so.

"I thought you wouldn't, when you told me you were going," said Mr. Black. "He is very blunt now and then. He sometimes gives me lectures on my duty as a landlord, and they are very amusing. I like him very much. He is a most original character. We have never had a teacher anything like him here. The earnings of the school are remarkably high for its size, and he has stimulated the other teachers in the parish greatly. He has constantly urged on me the policy of raising salaries and so commanding the services of better men and women, a policy of which I personally have certainly seen the benefit, for the rates are lower by a good deal now than they have ever been before and they are steadily going down. Besides, it is education he is aiming at and not cram. He is an excellent fellow. I do hope we shall manage to keep him here."

"What did he say to you?" he added; but he saw that Mr. Mann was taking the matter rather more seriously than he had expected, for he believed that Mr. Mann at bottom had lurking doubts on many points although he seemed so calm and proper. He took his eyes off the minister's face.

"He refused to come," returned Mr. Mann, avoiding more detail.

"Yes, I hope we shall manage to keep him here," said Mr. Black, fully conscious that Mr. Mann did not wish to go into the subject further, and desiring to assist him, "and I think we may, for I believe he is very fond of his pretty cousin down at Taft."

Mr. Mann felt pained to find that his infirmity of blushing came upon him now. He glanced at Miss Black. Her eyes were on him, and there was a puzzled expression in them.

Late that evening, he stood a long while in his bed-room window, thinking, and his eyes were on the little window in the south gable of the house at Taft.

CHAPTER IX

THROUGH MIST

"Le cœur a ses raisons que la raison ne connait point."—PASCAL

NEXT day, which was Sunday, Hakki left the Schoolhouse in the evening and went down to Taft. He had been at Taft the previous Sunday, but he had not got a chance of seeing Inga by herself. Bob had not been there, for a thick fog had kept him at the fishing station, fuming at the hindrance in a way that only Magni Sharp could fully understand, although Young Erti had "a sort of a kind of a notion" of it, as he muttered to himself when he observed Bob's angry, disappointed face.

"Well?" said Hakki as he walked into the parlour and found Inga sitting there alone. "What's du efter now, Inga?"

"What am I efter? " repeated Inga, looking up from a piece of sewing she was doing, and feeling rather nervous and defiant, for she knew a lecture was about to follow. "Du can see what I'm efter, glied [squint-eyed] as du is."

Hakki gave one of his short laughs.

"Dat's a brilliant bit o repartee for a peerie lass like dee," he said, "but very dangerous, my dear, very dangerous. Bairns should never play wi sharp things."

He flung himself down on the bulky, haircloth sofa, and looked across at her, his pipe going full blast.

"Yes?" said Inga ironically.

"Yes, very dangerous," continued Hakki, "and I'll tell dee why. It's because du's turnin glied in a far worse way diself."

"What does du mean, Hakki?" she asked in a sharp, injured tone, and putting on a very innocent air. She felt inclined to jump up and run from the room; but her pride prevented her from beating a retreat.

"So glied, in fact," pursued Hakki imperturbably, "that du can't see plain duty, even when it's right before dy very short and somewhat imperfectly-formed nose."

"Now, dat's not fair, Hakki," said Inga, bending her head over her sewing again.

"No, I suppose du thinks not," laughed Hakki, "but it's curious that, my jewel, for du seems to think everything fair if it only happens to suit diself."

"I'm heard o Saatan reprovin sin," she said, with a little laugh.

"It's a point in his favour if he did," said Hakki, "but I believe it was the nature of women that first suggested the Devil fable to men's minds. When a woman is in anything the Devil is never far away."

In his didactic moods, his dropping of the dialect entirely usually showed that he meant serious business.

"Da first woman wis a piece o a man," retorted Inga mischievously.

"The worst piece," said Hakki bitterly. "The old Jews had sensible ideas about women. It has been reserved for Christianity to make angels of them and fools of them at the same time. But to come to the present; can du tell me why it was du sent Lowra Sharp to take the sewing in the school last week and this week too, and never came diself?"

"Lowra took it for me da whole time I wis in Fetlar. Shö's da same as me," said Inga, without looking up.

"It would be too much to expect a straight answer from a woman," said Hakki, "even from a young woman, yes, even from a red-haired woman, and a woman with a disappointing nose. But, as a mere possibility, can du tell me why du didn't come?"

He had teased Inga mercilessly about her nose since the time she was twelve and had one night put a clothespin on it, because she had been anxious even then to look her best and had thought that it was too broad at the point.

"Dat's my business, not dine," returned Inga irritably.

"Is it?" said Hakki in a biting tone. "I'm afraid it's more people's business than either dine or mine. I suppose du doesn't see that there is any other body in it."

"Well, what business is dat o dine?" asked Inga cuttingly and glancing at him as she spoke.

"In one sense, none," returned Hakki coolly, "but in the interest of humanity in general, and of one good man in particular, a very great deal."

Inga was hurt at his cold tone. She saw that any feeling he had had for her a little stronger than the merely cousinly was nothing to him at the present moment, and it pained her vanity to think that this was so.

"Once upon a time du widna have said dat," she said watching him from under her lashes.

Hakki laughed.

"O, I thought so," he said, mockingly. "Always the cloven foot. Du couldn't forget that, even for a moment, in order to talk seriously. That means, of course, that du can't forgive my present attitude. I observed before that du was turning morally 'glied.' I suppose du couldn't manage to stick to the point for a little, merely as a personal favour. No. When women get logical, we shall, I daresay, have the Millenium, with all the benefits which in this life do either accompany or flow from it. Eh? Does du think du can tell me yet why du didn't come up to the school?"

Inga could scarcely master her vexation. She dropped her eyes again.

"Du taalks as if du knew all aboot it," she said quietly; but her hand shook on her sewing.

If Hakki had been gentler with her then, there would have been less pain to suffer in the time to come; but Fate has no subjunctive mood. He always aimed more at the head than at the heart. From disposition and from training this was natural to him.

"Yes, and du talks as if du knew nothing about it," he said bitterly. "I suppose it will be necessary to make things extremely plain. I suppose I shall have to tell dee why du didn't come up to the school."

"Du can save diself da trouble," said Inga sharply. "I'm no comin ta da school again. I saw Mr. Black aboot it dis forenoon, an Lowra is ta go instead o me."

She looked steadily at him as she spoke.

He had seen Mr. Black and Mr. Mann go north along together that forenoon, apparently for a short walk. They had been at the shop. For a moment his own feeling, that had been stimulated to a quicker life when Mr. Mann had blushed on seeing Inga's photograph upon the mantelpiece, pressed painfully on him, and he asked himself why Inga had not mentioned Mr. Mann as well as Mr. Black. But this only made him more sarcastic, for he knew that he had settled this thing in his mind, that he was now in a final way Bob's advocate, that the motive urging him was his conviction of the moral right Bob had to Inga's love. He had smoked a good few pipes of Faithful Lover before reaching that conclusion; but he had got there at last.

"O, yes," he said, meeting her steady look, with a queer smile on his face; "I suppose that'll leave dee freer to look after any little bits of engineering shortly to begin."

"Look here, Hakki, stop it," said Inga quickly.

"O, yes; stop it," he said banteringly. "Admirably feminine. Du would like me to stop it before I have ever begun it. I am just going to commence now. It would be better for dee if du was actually just going to commence too. But the commencement is over. It occurred the Sunday before last, or possibly the Sunday before that. The question is now—what next?"

Inga let her sewing drop in her lap. She leaned her elbow on the table, and her chin upon her hand and sat looking across at Hakki.

"In the first place," he went on, "I did not think that du was mean; in the second place, I thought du had a heart; and, in the third place, I believed du had sufficient common sense to see that there is quite enough confusion in the world already without dee trying to make more. Being a woman, or to speak more properly, a girl, du will naturally consider these things immaterial. Being a man, I, of course, consider them very material indeed, especially in the case of Bob, for instance."

She saw plainly that he had no thought of bringing in himself. His tone was cold and hurt her, for under all her vanity her heart was warm and loving. It cut her so much that she felt inclined to cry, as she had been used to do when she was small and Hakki teased her, at which times Hakki had been wont to come and kiss her and make all right again. But they were not children now. Her pride told her she should show him, now, that she was independent, told her that he was unreasonable and too severe, that she had really not deserved so much. Her clear brain, which intercourse with Hakki had stirred to keenest life, told her that she was wrong, that Hakki had always been her hero, that his mental loneliness and the strength of purpose with which he went on his own way bending gradually in spite of opposition the whole district to his will, had touched her heart and struck her reason powerfully; but the personality of Mr. Mann had somehow touched her heart still more, and Hakki's words had just that moment wounded her, and had let her very clearly understand that his life did not actually need her. The heart has its own laws and in a woman feeling is usually mistress of conviction. The thought of Hakki's plain indifference once more pained her, and stung her pride. His next words made her angry.

"Novelty is generally entertaining," he went on. "It is interesting to see a person we thought sensible behaving like a fool."

"Yes, it is," said Inga, in a bitter tone. "I wis jöst noticin it nu."

"It's a pity du didn't notice it rather sooner," said Hakki, with a cold smile; "but the point is this: if du has come to think that du can really care for Bob, then, in Heaven's name, show him some affection in return for the true, strong love that he has wasted upon dee; but if du sees du cannot care for him as he deserves, in God's name, tell him plainly, for du knows nothing of the agony a man like him can suffer if he is deceived."

The last word cut her like a knife. Tears of vexation would have come now certainly, if it had not been for her pride.

"I'll do exactly as I please," she said, angrily, and her tone was very hard.

Hakki laughed, jumped up from the bulky sofa, and began walking backwards and forwards across the floor behind her chair. Once or twice she thought that he was going suddenly to stop at her back and put his arms about her, and she sat ready to resent it; but he did not stop. He did not even speak for a good while, then all at once he said abruptly,

"Don't du lead Bob along a heavenly way to Hell; a hellish way to Heaven would be better. Is Uncle in the shop?"

He went out, smoking fiercely.

She did not know that every time he had walked past behind her he had watched her rounded bosom heaving and had wished with all his might he could have felt it heaving so, with love, against his own.

In the shop he found Hansi and Willa in past the counter. Aald Erti was the only customer. Hakki went in past and spoke to Hansi for a little, then he bought some matches and turned to go again.

"Du's no goin hom yit, boy," said Willa, wondering at his unusual abruptness.

"I'll be down to-morrow," he said as he went out. Aald Erti hurried after him. Outside the mist was like a hedge.

"It's as thick as pea-soup," he said.

"Yes, sir; it is that, sir," returned Erti, jerkily; "but I seen it worse, sir, when I was out in Canady, I seen it so thick that we could hear it scrapin on the loghouse we was in, sir, as it was a-blowin past, sir."

They passed the parlour window.

Inga had shifted to the bulky sofa, for the fog had made the room quite dim. She saw them going by.

If Hakki had looked round, had even sent one glance towards the window, she felt she could have pardoned him the harshness of his words; but he walked past stiff and straight and did not turn his head, his strong, clean-made figure contrasting forcibly with Erti's cringing person.

"I've seen it worse than that at sea," said Hakki wickedly, for he usually gave Aald Erti change on such occasions. "One voyage to Halifax we ran full butt into a fogbank and carried away our jibboom."

"Exackly so, sir; I seen the very same," said Erti heartily.

"Yes," said Hakki, "and the infernal thing was so hard that we had to land on it with hatchets and cut out an anchor hold. We had to moor up to it, for we couldn't face it, and in two days the wind was round due east and we and the whole show drove into Halifax, and the bank was cut up and sold for building purposes."

"Ta be sure, sir," said Erti.

They turned up along the south side of the yard.

At that moment Bob Ertirson was coming down along the north side of the yard.

"I'm going to Hooll," said Hakki, quickening his pace.

"So am I, sir," said Erti, almost running to keep up with him; "yes, in a menner of speakin. I generally goes hom past Hooll, sir. It's not so disconvennient. We had the minister along, sir, at Vatster the other day, askin Erti and Janny, sir, to come and taech in the Sunday school there, as it were, sir; but I thinks with you, sir, as how there's too much of them religious things agoing on nowadays and a damned sight too little honesty, sir, and such like, among the people. Yes, sir; that night I heerd you talkin with old Magnus Sharp, as is a clever owld man for his chances, I seen things clearer, in a menner of speakin, sir. I seen as how there was certain duties, yes, as a man was bound to do, because they was right and nobble, sir, and I tells you open like, as how them words o yours done me more good, sir, 'pun mi sowl, sir, as any hunder sermons I ever heerd, and that's the God's truth, sir. You haven't got a bit of baccy on you, sir?"

When they got to Hooll, Erti kept on for Vatster; but Hakki opened the door of old Magnus' workshop and went in. He was surprised to find Magni sitting there beside his father. There was a small fire on the hearth for the fog had made the evening chilly, and old Magnus had to watch himself for rheumatism. Magnus and Magni were sitting, one on each side of the chimney, smoking. They usually had quiet cracks together in the workshop of an evening before going finally into the house.

"Hallo, Magni," said Hakki as he entered, "I didn't know du had come home this Helly."

"Me an Bob cam haem aboot a 'oor ago," said Magni, pulling in a stool for Hakki.

"Well, old Father Wax, what news?" said Hakki, tapping old Magnus on the shoulder, and sitting down.

Old Magnus laughed and rubbed his hands. Nothing delighted him more than a visit from Hakki. He used to say it cheered him more than a good stiff glass of whisky.

"News?" cried he. "Owld Solomon says at dere's nothin new under da sun; bit feth! I tink he surely never hed rheumatics. Der alwas somethin new wi rheumatics. It's a winderful cheery thing, if a body onnly hed time ta notice it. It begins i your shouder, an ye're sittin winderin what'll be best ta dö for it, whin ye notice at it's shiftit ta da sma o your back. An ye begin ta try an mind da kinds o things at idder folk is gotten göd wi usin, whin ye finn at it's no dere at aal bit i your limb. It's a kind o secind cousin ta da Deevil, feth, I tink; or it's been mairried on his aant, or been some wy conneckit wi da faimily, for it's aye goin aboot laek a lion seekin whom it may devour; an it doesna roar, na, dat's da warst o it, or a pör body micht manage ta escape. Na, na, it's you at haes ta dö da roarin."

"Have you been eating onions, as I bade you?" asked Hakki with a laugh, "and drinking that lemon-juice I sent you, regularly?"

"Na; raelly I forgot," replied old Magnus.

"Then the Devil help you, you old sinner," said Hakki with a smile; "you're a stiffnecked and rebellious generation."

"Ye mann pardon me for dis time," laughed old Magnus.

"Ask you your shoulder and your back and your limb to pardon you," said Hakki, "and repent at once. I believe in instantaneous conversion on a point like this. You tell Lowra to give you some of your medicine before you turn in, or I'll talk to you, my man."

Old Magnus chuckled.

"Bi mi sang! ye wid 'a made a faerce doctor, if ye hed taen efter bottles instead o efter books," he said.

Hakki turned to Magni.

"So Bob and dee came home by land," he said. "Yea," answered Magni.

Hakki saw a look upon his face, that he had never noticed there before.

"I wid laek ta spaek wi you a moment," added Magni.

"I'll tell Lowra aboot yon at wance," said old Magnus, with a delicacy that was natural to him. He got up and went into the house.

"Did ye no meet Bob?" asked Magni as the old man closed the door.

"No," answered Hakki, with his eyes on Magni's face.

"He's awey doon ta Taft," said Magni slowly. He sat looking into the fire.

"I understand," said Hakki quietly.

"I'm never seen him laek what he's been for da past fortnight," said Magni, a little hesitatingly. "I dont know what he'll do, if things go wrang wi him doon yonder. What I wis goin ta say is dis, an I know ye'll understaand me, or I widna spaek; could ye no help him some wy, tink ye?"

Magni's usual jollity was gone. He raised his eyes and looked at Hakki. In that look Hakki read at once that Magni had long stood his ground against temptation and had triumphed.

"Yes," said Magni, and his strong, deep voice was low and tender, "he's da truest sowl I ever knew. God help him, if he haes ta suffer more dan he haes hed ta suffer for da past tree year."

Hakki saw that Magni had done more than he had done, already. He suddenly held out his hand to him.

When Bob got down behind the house at Taft he hesitated for a moment. Then a vague impulse sent him round the south end of the house and past the parlour window.

Inga heard his footsteps and looked up. He saw her at the window, and stood still. At the sudden sight of Bob standing there so strong and big against the mist, with his hot heart in his eyes, a strange feeling came upon her. She was still smarting under Hakki's words. Two or three times since Hakki had marched from the room she had made up her mind to do as he had told her, to tell Bob plainly that she did not care for him, that her new kindness to him had been nothing but a passing whim. She had thought that Bob would probably be home next week, and that would give her time to nerve herself, for she knew that it would be very hard for her to let him know that she had, even slightly, played with him. But Hakki's coolness had provoked her so that she was not in a mood to follow his advice, and now Bob stood before her, and she scarcely knew what she should do. After the first momentary shock, the thought that he was there was pleasant to her. He had always been so good a soul and so invariably gentle. After Hakki's biting words, Bob's presence brought a sense of comfort. Without further thought she smiled to him, and pointed to the porch.

Next minute she met him at the room door.

"Come in, boy," she said. In her excited state of feeling her tone was full of eager kindliness. It swept clean from Bob's mind the doubts and the suspicions that had tortured him through all that fortnight. A rush of gladness almost overpowered him as he caught the tone. His strong love lifted him, for that brief moment, out of his reserve and fear of her. Before she knew what he was going to do, he seized her in his arms and kissed her passionately.

CHAPTER X

THE WORKERS

"Let not Ambition mock their useful toil."—GRAY

"ARE you feeling unwell, Peter?" asked Mrs. Mann anxiously, one day at dinner two months later.

"No, mother," answered Mr. Mann; "why do you ask?"

"Because you are looking paler than you usually do, and some days you go so often to your room. You seem very much preoccupied; at times, I almost think, depressed," she said.

He looked at her somewhat wearily, as if he had grown sick of some of his own thoughts and scarcely cared to trouble speaking of them; but the anxious look he saw upon her face made him try to relieve her by explaining things a little way.

"I have been feeling rather restless and dissatisfied of late," he said, "and the habit of wandering through the house has grown upon me. I think I shall have my writing-table shifted upstairs to my bedroom for a time. It is cheerier there, where one looks out upon the hill-side and the sky and sea. I have grown sick of staring through the study window at the garden wall.

He did not tell her that he had for weeks been trying to resist the subtle influence that he felt Inga gaining over him, and that in spite of all his efforts it was growing stronger every day, had grown so strong, in fact, that he had planned to write upstairs where he could look sometimes at Taft without the need of wandering through the house as he had done.

"Well, that can easily be done," said Mrs. Mann, "if you think it will be better. You can get the two young men, Bob Ertirson and Magni Sharp, to lift it up for you. It's rather heavy for the girls to work with, you know. Bob and Magni will be home perhaps tomorrow. Jeems Ertirson was here this morning with a present of potatoes for us, and he was telling Naanie that he thought Bob would be home to-morrow, for the weather has become so broken that they will not think there's any use of fishing longer. I'll send word to Jeems to-night, and he will tell Bob and Magni.

"Very well," said Mr. Mann; but he felt that he would rather have had two different men.

"You have thought I looked at times depressed," he went on. "Well, I have felt sometimes depressed. For six months I have been slaving here, yes, spiritually and mentally slaving, and the whole place seems to lie as dead as on the day I entered it."

His tone was wearied, querulous, and almost bitter. She had never heard him talk like that before. To her anxious ears there seemed to be in the tone a faint but noticeable echo of his father's violence of temper. This was the mood that had been wont to go along with heavy drinking bouts. She thanked God that her son, as far as she knew, had never tasted drink. But his tone filled her with a vague sense of apprehension.

"It is God's work, Peter," she said gently, "and you do not have to do it in your own strength alone."

"I know that well enough," he said, almost pettishly, "but I am talking of the result as it reveals itself at present. It is not at all encouraging to see that all a man's best thought and energy must go to do no more than tickle curious ears."

"Your work is of a deeper sort than that," she said in her sweet voice, which usually soothed him more than any other; but its effect was growing weaker as other influences strengthened.

"I do not value popularity a straw," continued he, "what I desire to see is quickened spiritual and moral life in every household in the parish as the natural and necessary fruit of the Good Seed that I have sown. I wish to see men, sceptical and negligent before, acknowledging the power and grandeur of the Gospel; but there is Perk, for instance, and there is old Magnus Sharp. I might as well have spoken to the wind. Perk simply laughs at me, and I suspect old Magnus does the same."

"The spirit of God can deal with them also," said Mrs. Mann reverently. "'Rest in the Lord and wait patiently for Him and He will give thee thy heart's desire.'"

They rose from the table and Mr. Mann went into his study for his usual after-dinner smoke; but he had not been long there till he came out again and went upstairs.

He had not told his mother what had happened last time he had called on Hakki and old Magnus; but he was thinking now of both these interviews, as he went up to his own room to stand there at the window for a while and smoke and look across at Taft.

Hakki had said, in his usual, incisive manner,

"Give the people science, sound and certain knowledge about life in all its aspects, and leave off bothering about your Eschatology and other mediæval rubbish. The world has no time left for superstition now. If the present life is right, a future life, if there be one, can not by any possibility be wrong. Teach the people to do right and give up trying to frighten them with bogies. God's idea is development. Stick you to that, and let Him balance His own books Himself; He'll manage it without your aid. That's Faith, with a vengeance. The Faith you talk about is blarney. Three-fourths of its time is wasted speculating and poking around where it has no business, sticking its eye to the keyhole of Heaven to try and find out what the Eternal means to do about the business finally. Haul off your coat and go straight at the facts, and let the theories go to the Devil."

He had answered firmly,

"The knowledge of Jesus Christ and Him crucified is the best of all science. Each soul enlightened by His Spirit will endeavour to do right. The gospel is the power of God unto salvation."

"Salvation from what?" Hakki had asked. "Take any average Christian church and watch the petty jealousies and spitefulnesses you will find especially among the women in it, and the pure and saintly way in which the male professors carry on their ordinary business, and then tell me what it is these people have been saved from. Their bargain will be very good indeed if they are ultimately saved from that hot Hell you are so fond of talking of. I suppose that's what they're counting on. But if that's all your Christianity can do, it's time the world had a shot at something else."

"You are unfair," he had replied. "You ask perfection, and yet you tell me God's idea is development. Do you call that logical?"

"God's idea is one thing," Hakki had returned, "and the idea of your mediæval scholasticism is quite another. These people have new hearts; they have been washed in the blood of the Lamb; they at stated periods feed upon Him; one really would expect them to do something even brilliant after such a process."

"They do," he had replied. "It is useless to dispute the patent fact of saintly lives. You have no right to gauge a church by a selection of its weakest members."

"They are supposed to be new creatures," Hakki had retorted. "I fail to see their right to this poor, human perquisite of weakness."

"I have known those who did not need to urge the right," he had replied.

"Perhaps you would not care to give an estimate of the percentage," Hakki had said.

"The working of God's Spirit is a mystery," he had said. "No man can measure its unseen and mighty power."

"Yes, it is a mystery," Hakki had retorted viciously, "and its mighty power is really very difficult to measure, especially when one finds it doesn't have sufficient influence over its own ministers to save them from behaving foolishly to the first pretty girl that they chance to come across, even when their tender trifling means the torture of a truer heart."

He had felt this to be such gross impertinence that he had not replied, and they had parted very coldly.

When he had visited old Magnus, he had found the old man in his usual humour of mingled playfulness and cynicism.

"Na, na, sir," he had answered with a chuckle, jerking his blue elbows out as he sat stitching; "ye needna fash yoursell wi askin me ta come doon ta da kirk or ta your weeknicht meetins. I hae my aald Bible here apo da shelf, an I tink it's da same kind o ean as ye hae. I'm greatly obleedged ta da laerned men 'at set it ower frae da Hebra an da Greek ta da Engleis for da laeks o me; an it's braa muckle print 'at I can manage fine. Keep ye your kirk for dem at canna read an tink; bit come up alang, O yea, come up alang, for I'm blyde ta see you as a freend, ye ken. O yea; dat am I; dat am I indeed. Ye're young, ye see; bit ye'll learn, my lamb, ye'll learn; dat'll ye. I'll aye be sayin a wird ta you nu an dan. Did ye hear da news, sir?"

"News?" Mr. Mann had echoed. "What news?"

"Ye ken Oli Jarmson?" old Magnus had said, looking keenly up with the pucker on his face.

"Yes, perfectly," he had replied. "What is it about him?"

"It's very tryin, sir, very tryin indeed," Magnus had said, still watching him.

"What is it, Magnus?" he had demanded.

"A wumman hed a child till him last nicht, sir," Magnus had answered.

Mr. Mann had been horrorstruck, for Oli was one of his most esteemed kirk-members.

"What woman, Magnus?" he had faintly asked.

"His wife, sir," old Magnus had solemnly replied, and Mr. Mann had gone away hopelessly, leaving Magnus chuckling,

"Bi mi sang, I tink dat did him," as before.

Mr. Mann had made the mistake of getting his new boots from Lerwick.

From his window he looked out across the short, green slope above the kirk, the dark strip of heather from which the purple bloom was slowly fading, and the corn of Taft, which was beginning to be cut that day. He saw the folk there in the "rig," Jeems Ertirson, Aald Erti Gair, and Hendri Jeemson, with Ann Ertirson, Janny Gair, Lowra Sharp, and Betty Jeemson. The feeling of regret that autumn often brings did not in any way affect him. He had grown weary of the summer. He felt it was the summer that had killed his work, that it had filled the minds of folk with earthly cares, with thoughts about their fishings and their crops, that they had little interest in the church and in his work at such a season. The big attendance at the kirk had fallen off. Folk from a distance, having been and heard the man about whom everyone was talking, were quite satisfied and did not come again. The interest in the Sunday school had not at all grown as he had at first hoped, though he had certainly observed a small improvement. The days had dragged. He had felt the German readings would have been some slight relief; but Mr. Black had said that there was no use starting till October. He saw that most things went on quietly in the place, just as they likely had been going all the time, though he had thought at first that he had made a very noticeable difference. Mr. Black, he might say, was polite towards the church, but nothing more. He took no interest in religious matters. He would not put himself about. His wife was little better. Her interest was principally theoretical. Miss Black, however, had been prompt to help in every way she could.

"Perhaps Miss Black was right," he said to himself, "and my ideal is impossible."

He had thought often of her words, and of the sympathy she had so readily accorded. But the coming winter might bring keener interest in the church and in the meetings he had planned to start just the next week. He felt he did not care much at the present moment.

He was really wondering if it would not be much better to be quiet, to settle down to ordinary humdrum work as other men had had to do before, to preach perfunctorily his sermon on the Sundays and interest himself in farming through the week. He could not just now bear the thought that this was to be all. But he thought next moment that it actually mattered very little. He could not hide from himself the fact that Inga's influence over him had grown more rapidly of late, as he had felt less interest in his work, and his face flushed as he thought that he was glad the evenings had grown longer, so that he could now more easily drop in at Taft without exciting gossip on the line of Hakki's violent hint. He went to Taft ostensibly to talk with Hansi, his chief elder. But he knew well enough that it was Inga he was anxious to see. Willa's eyes, though they were not so good as they had been, were keen enough to see a thing like that, and she had several times with great art spoken to him as her godly minister about her own anxiety for Inga's future, telling him that her maternal love could not endure the thought of seeing Inga married to a man like Bob, who was and would be nothing but a fisherman and crofter, when Inga was so clever and had got some education and her father was worth a good deal of money. She had told him too that the feeling was entirely on Bob's side, and that Inga did not really care for Bob, a statement he had seen no cause to doubt.

He had felt sorry for Bob certainly; but he had told himself that it was natural for Inga to feel as she did. Bob had sometimes been rather cold to him of late; but he said to himself he could not help it.

He turned from the window, took a chair and placed it so that when he sat down on it he could still see Taft quite comfortably, and that was how he meant his writing-table to be placed.

He did not go to Taft that evening; but when he had gone upstairs for the night he stood a long while at the window looking across at the white gable in the moonlight. Then he pulled down the blind and went to bed.

He was awakened early in the morning by hearing voices underneath his window, which he had left a little open from the top. He recognised them as the voices of John Jarmson, Aald Erti Gair, and Hendri Jeemson, who had now snatched a day to come and point the gable.

"Well, men," said Aald Erti importantly (he was the man that mixed lime for the others); "do ye think he's goin to be anything of a day for it? There's a nasty lump of him up there in the south-west."

"Weel, my lamb, I never ken," said old John slowly. "At dis time o year he sometimes traetens a lok an it comes ta naething."

"Dat so," said Hendri Jeemson, in a solemn tone, and with great deliberation.

Hendri had never been known to run except on one occasion.

"Well, John," said Aald Erti, carefully scanning the heavens, in which task he was aided by the other two; "if he's not goin to be a day it would be a pity to wrastle with the gavel at all, for if we have to knock off it'll relly be very anonymous."

"Dat so," said Hendri solemnly.

"Whereby," continued Erti, "if we dont make a start there's no harm done, in a menner of speakin, and we is saved from the disconvennience of bein laid to the hide with rain, should he once lowse."

"Yea, dat's true," said John, turning from scanning the heavens to scan the gable of the house; "bit I tink we'll mak a beginning; we hae da ledders up, an he's laek ta be moaderate for a while."

"Dat so," said Hendri.

"Ta be sure," said Erti.

Old John straightened his rheumatic angle as far as he was able, and then looked about him.

"Is everything here nu, men?" he asked. "I see no bucket for da watter. Broucht du ean, Erti?"

Erti had not brought one, for he had meant to borrow one from the servants in the Manse, and afterwards, if possible, remove it west to Vatster as a perquisite.

"No, John," he said largely, "I see I've admitted to bring a bucket; but they'll have one for the most part in the house here, and I'll go and attain it from the servant lass."

"Der ean at Hooll," said Hendri in a grave, slow tone, which clearly showed he was best man to go for it if the work was to be paid for by the hour.

The advantage of despatching Hendri for it seemed to strike old John; but such a serious step could not be taken without previous discussion.

After a patient debate, extending over about twenty minutes, in the course of which the geographical position of the bucket was ascertained approximately, old John summed up and said that Hendri might take a look the length of Hooll, and, if he found the bucket there, bring it down with him "in his haand," though Hendri had no wish to carry it in any other way. So Hendri started at a pace so thoroughly his own that it seemed some time before he got away from the immediate neighbourhood of his companions, while Aald Erti, not to be baulked of the prey he scented in the other bucket, started for the Manse kitchen door. When Hendri got to Hooll he found that his wife Betty, who hated all unseemly haste as much as he did, had just risen and was making tea, of which she wished him to enjoy a cup before undertaking his arduous return journey to the Manse. Aald Erti sat down by the Manse kitchen fire to light his pipe, while old John lit his with a match outside and stood examining the heavens. When they assembled again, about three-quarters of an hour afterwards, Mr. Mann had risen and was putting on his clothes.

"Well, John," said Aald Erti, "I'll perceed up the ledder for the more security, and see that the block is all right."

"I think this is the window of the room that he sleeps in," he said as he got near the top, and tried to peer in at the edge of the blind, which Mr. Mann had not yet raised. "I see a fine basin-stand there, and a kist of drawers. Yes, feth, he dont want for nothing. Them things'll cost some pounds, in a menner of speakin, and it's the likes of us as has got to sweat for it. Yes, it's the poor as has to siffer, and the ministers is cled in fine linen and fares scrumptiously every day, as the Scripters says. And owld Mann's bit o boy can lie in his bed till ten o'clock in the morning, and the likes of me which his owld drukken father made his money off has to be toiling and slaving like this. But there's a day of recknin coming; yes, there's a day of recknin."

Hendri slowly climbed the other ladder, while old John went round to the kitchen porch to fetch his trowel.

"Dat so," said Hendri solemnly.

"They tell me," went on Aald Erti, when old John was gone, "that Mann here is making a kind of sweethearting of Hansi Bolt's red-headed lass, but I dont know to the truth of it, and that she's holding up with Bob Ertirson too. This Mann is foolich enough. Look at the way he's working with this glibe of his, with none to see after it but owld John's son Oli, as hasn't no more brains as a hen."

Mr. Mann winced as he stood inside listening. Then he suddenly pulled up the blind and Erti rapidly removed his eye. Mr. Mann opened the window and looked out.

"Good morning," said he.

"O, good mornin, sir," said Erti jerkily. "I was just sayin, sir, as how we was all glad to see you so comfortable in the house like, sir, for the brainwork is the hardest of the lot, sir, and no mistake. And I was just sayin as how it was time you was a-sweetheartin some of the young ladies hereabout like Miss Black or Miss Bolt, sir,—beg pardon, sir; but it's a netural thing that you should settle down, sir. And I was just sayin as how it was a graet comfort to see the glibe lookin so well and that you have the like of Oli menaging it, for you might have had a man as hadn't no more brains as a hen. Yes, sir. Them was my words, sir, and Hendri here'll tell you the very same."

"Dat so," said Hendri solemnly.

"Will you finish the gable to-day?" asked Mr. Mann stiffly.

"Well, sir," said Erti, with a philosophical little laugh, "there's many things connectit with all things, in a menner of speakin; and that's more as I could say. But I think we'll perhaps come to a collusion with the gavel this evening, sir, for the most part, or somewhere before denner-time to-morrow. It's a nasty lump of a gavel, sir, as you sees, sir, but we is pushin on as fast as possible. We're going to be at your corn to-morrow, sir. Oli is anxious to have the west rig cut at once, sir, and it's a da-da-daeshed pity, sir,—beg pardon, sir,—that the corn wasn't cut sooner, sir, when the wedder is so oon-dependable. When I had the glibe it was all snug and tidy by this time, sir. Just the other day I says to Oli, I says, says I, 'Oli—'"

But Mr. Mann had left the window.

In the afternoon Bob and Magni came to lift the writing-table upstairs from the study to the bedroom. As they waited in the study for Mr. Mann, who was upstairs, to come down to them, Magni said to Bob that he felt as if Bob was now bridegroom and himself best-man, and that they had come to the Manse to speak to Mann about the banns. Bob smiled. It seemed to him a pleasant omen, for he was for the moment in a hopeful mood and glad that he was now home for the winter. After his passionate kiss, his fear of Inga had returned; but he had felt better than before, for she was still kindly in her manner to him, though at times a little whimsical, he thought. He had been pretty fairly satisfied, for in the light of his new hope he felt that he could overlook a good few little things. He did not know that what was making Inga act so was the fact that she had never yet found courage to speak plainly to him, and her pity for him was becoming greater every day.

When they had got the table up and set it where Mann wanted it, they found they had forgotten the screw-driver in the room below, and the minister went down to get it. Magni sat down at the writing-table, spread his elbows on it, stuck out his tongue, and said to Bob:

"What wy, tinks du, wid I shape at writin sermons, boy?"

As he raised his head he noticed all at once that he was looking right at Taft, and an unwelcome explanation of this flitting struck him; but he did not speak to Bob about it.

Mr. Mann came back, and Bob took from his pocket a letter he had brought from Taft and gave it to the minister. It had come with the post that day.

Bob and Magni left, and Mr. Mann sat down at his table and opened his epistle. It was from two evangelists, Mr. Thomas Howell and Mr. John Meek, asking if he would let them have the use of his church for a series of gospel meetings to be held in the first fortnight of December.

That evening he went over to Taft to see what Hansi thought of this. But Hansi was west in the parish buying sheep, and he found Inga in the shop alone. Everybody in the place was busy with their crops, or other things. There was a certain shyness in the way that Inga greeted him, a shyness which he felt attracted him most powerfully. He meant to buy a tweed cap that would stop on better than his hat, now when the days were getting windy, and Inga took the rickety shop-steps and went to lift a bandbox with the caps down from the highest shelf.

"These steps are not very steady," he said with a smile. "I'll hold them for you, or perhaps you'll fall."

She blushed and smiled and thanked him, and he came in past, and held the steps. He saw her neat, little ankles with the brown stockings, and her pretty feet with their small shoes. It thrilled him through and through to be so near her. He felt that he would rather hold herself than hold the steps. She reached up for the bandbox, but in her nervousness she pulled it down so quickly that she let it go, then made a clutch at it and lost her balance. She came right down into the arms of Mr. Mann, and buried her nose in his bosom. He felt her hair brush past his cheek and tickle him, and she felt his moustache against her brow and tickling her. A strong temptation seized him to hold her on and kiss her wildly.

Just then he heard the shuffling of a pair of "rivlined" feet upon the shop floor at his back. Inga instantly released herself. They both looked round and saw that it was Janny Gair.

CHAPTER XI

JACOB

"Tis sweet to know there is an eye will mark

Our coming, and look brighter when we come."—BYRON

"I AM glad I saved you from a fall, Miss Bolt," said Mr. Mann, thinking it best to face the situation promptly. But he felt that he was flushing, and he bent to lift the bandbox from the floor.

"Yes, thank you," answered Inga hastily. "I was very near away."

She too bent to lift the bandbox, and they knocked their heads together. Both laughed nervously. They did not seem to hurry getting up the box. At last Mr. Mann lifted it, set it on the counter, and came out past.

"Good evening, Janet," said he, holding out his hand, and feeling only slightly comforted to think that it was dusk. "Miss Bolt has very nearly had a fall. I am glad I caught her just in time."

"I daarsay," said Janny, but she gave no further sign.

She felt she had been witness to a little incident that, as a bit of scandal, could be made quite succulent, and was well worthy of her most artistic treatment.

"Will du gie me a onnce o tay wi di haand, Inga?" she said instantly.

She seemed in no way anxious to inflict her presence on them longer than was necessary.

Inga felt at once the plain insinuation this implied.

"Du's no in a hurry, lass," she said, recovering herself, and feeling eager now to checkmate Janny. "I was just goin ta let Mester Mann see some caps, an dan I'll get it ta dee."

Janny saw she had lost the move.

Inga took the caps very deliberately out of the box, and spread them out for Mr. Mann to look at. He lifted one or two of them and took them to the door to look at. Then Inga calmly weighed the tea for Janny, who snatched the package up the moment Inga laid it on the counter.

"Mark it," she said, as she made for the door.

"God nicht, sir," she murmured with a smile, and brushed past Mr. Mann.

"O, good night, Janet," he responded thoughtfully, as he stood attentively examining the lining of a cap.

When Janny had got round the corner, he turned into the shop. Both he and Inga laughed nervously.

Inga was glad she had been able to act coolly before Janny; but now she felt confused, for the little accident had really given her more pleasure than she cared to show. She thought that Janny had just hurried off in order to let no grass grow under her red "rivlins" in the publication of her fresh bit of news, but she was not exactly right in this, for Janny was not quite in such a hurry; she had got a better notion. Inga felt she did not care, and she hoped he did not care; but his first words showed her that he did.

"I hope that girl will not go away and set the whole place talking," he said in a somewhat nervous tone.

Inga was disappointed, for she thought he would have laughed it off, and been too strong to mind the like of Janny; but now she felt that he was rather weaker than she had expected.

"I did not think that you would care," she said with a slight touch of her piqued manner. "What harm was in it?"

"O, none," he said, and he felt there was so little that he would have liked to take her in his arms again now that they were alone, if there had but been any feasible excuse for doing so. He felt his arms in fancy still about her and her full bosom pressing against his.

So strong a wave of feeling now came over him that his manner grew quite hesitating and abrupt. It passed through his mind that he must give the church to those evangelists.

Then Hansi turned the corner of the house and came into the shop.

"Weel, sir, what news?" said Hansi heartily, and they shook hands.

"Not much," he replied. "I was just buying a cap from Miss Bolt."

"That's right," said Hansi. "Did ye get da letter I sent ower ta you wi Bob?"

"I did," returned he, "and I came over to get your opinion about it. Here it is. You had better read it for yourself."

"Licht da lamp, Inga," said Hansi.

"I tink ye'll gie dem da kirk," he said, as soon as he had read the letter. "It cheers da place ta hae such meetins nu an dan."

Such meetings usually sent a good few folk along the shop.

"I am rather inclined to that view myself," he said; but he was really thinking about something else.

He turned to go. When he shook hands with Inga he gave her hand a warmer pressure than he had ever done before, and she forgave him for his nervousness.

At the Manse he found Young Erti waiting for him, and at first he felt a little startled, thinking that perhaps the quick departure Janny had made from the shop was in some way connected with this visit from her brother, though in what way he could not understand. But he was reassured when he had taken Erti to the study.

Aald Erti, anxious to make the visit of the minister to Vatster consistent with the dignity of the family, had told his son that Mr. Mann had come there specially to ask Young Erti to become a teacher in the Sunday school. Young Erti knew that Bob and Magni had been at the Manse that afternoon, and, knowing Bob had always been a teacher, he thought Bob had taken Magni over to the minister to get him made one too. He knew through Janny's vicious version of the interview at Vatster that the minister had got it all arranged that Inga was to be a teacher, and he did not mean to pass a chance like this, when he knew well enough that he could never have the chance Bob had of visiting her at Taft.

"Wal, sir," he said, sitting straight up in the chair Mr. Mann had given him and stroking his goatee beard with one hand, while he held his hard felt Sunday hat on his knee with the other, "I guess you was up at Vatster to see me one day but I warn't at home."

"Yes, I visited your father and sister," said Mr. Mann, "but knowing that you were away with the boat I did not expect to see you there. Did you wish to see me about anything?"

Erti cleared his throat impressively.

"Wal, sir," he said, "I've knocked araound a bit, and I believes in goin a thing straight. I understands as haow you wants me to come and give you a hand with that Sunday school of yours, and I hitches on naow, Sunday first, if you is agreeable."

The "Yenkee" fixed his sly, gray eyes sideways on Mr. Mann, without turning his face.

"I don't quite understand," said Mr. Mann.

"Wal," said Erti, thinking that the minister was perhaps in doubt regarding his attainments, "I dont pertend to be a edicated man, so far; but I seen as much as most, I reckon, and I knows all about Jirusalem and them places, sir. I got an old book in the house as I picked up in Shiels, and it's all about them places with charts of the whole blo-blessed show, sir. It stood me about three bob, it did; and I seen me spend a whole night a-studyin of it."

"O, yes," said Mr. Mann reflectively, for he was thinking more of Janny's knowledge than of Erti's.

"Yes, sir," continued Erti, with a Western emphasis on the "sir"; "I dont say as haow I'm particlar religious; but I'm down on them Jews as killed Jesus; thet's what I am, and I reckon thet's about the size of what you wants."

Mr. Mann coughed.

"Well, really," he said quietly, anxious to avoid unpleasantnesses, "I have not yet quite completed my arrangements for the Sabbath school; but it has not grown just so fast as I expected, and at present it does not actually need more teachers."

Erti thought he saw his drift. The implied refusal nettled him. There was an angry gleam in his sly gray eyes, but Mr. Mann did not see it.

"O, wal," he said, with a touch of sharpness in his tone, "of cowrse you knows best what you means to be after with it; but I tell you, you better watch yourself with some of them you've got naow. Megni Sharp ain't no good for the like of thet. He ain't been nowhere, excep two trips to Faera an wan to the West Ice. And he's a blo-blamed fool, into the bargain; anybody can see thet. But you picks your own friends, of cowrse; only, as a man thet's been raound a bit and seen things, I tells you straight, you better give the likes of him a wide berth, or, by the Lord Harry, you'll be a sheer hulk in about no time, in a place like this. Look at thet father of his, the old cobbler up there in Hooll, as ain't got no more religion as a grice [pig], and dont never go to no meetin; thet's about the kind of thing he's come of. He's a great lump of blasted impidence and egorince; thet's what he is. I can't open my mouth there in the boat, but what the big, ugly paws of him is floppin araound for a constancy. He dont know how to behave hisself. He's up and given me a slep on the beck sometimes, as nearly knocked me overboard. Of cowrse I could put him on the keel of his beck in two shakes; but I wouldn't dirty my hands with the likes of him. Thet's between ourselves like, for I dont expeck the likes of you, sir, to be goin repeatin my words and makin mischief in the place."

"Certainly not," said Mr. Mann, "but I think you do not quite understand. I have not asked Magni Sharp to come to the Sabbath school."

"O, I ain't quite so green, minister, by a long chalk, you bet," said Erti suspiciously. "Thet ain't just thick enough. Bob and him was raound here this afternoon."

"They were shifting a heavy piece of furniture for me."

"O, I see," said Erti slowly. "Wal, I didn't know thet, of cowrse."

"I shall be glad to see you at the week-night meetings that begin next week," said Mr. Mann. "I may be starting a Bible class to be held just after them, at which I also hope to see you present."

But Erti had set his mind on the Sunday school as suiting best his dignity and his designs.

"Wal, I'll see," he said, rising. "I can't exackly say nothin naow, till I sees haow it suits so far; but there ain't no blo-bloomin use of me hengin raound here and humbuggin longer to-night, espeecially when it's gettin on for your porridge time, so I guess I'll vamose the ranche, for the present. Evenin!"

He stuck his hard felt on over the bridge of his nose and turned to the door.

"I hope to see you again some evening," said Mr. Mann.

"O, yes," returned the "Yenkee" condescendingly, and feeling for the moment slightly mollified. "We'll give you a look in some evenin, and have a chet. It helps to pass the time like, and I tell you, I got some experriences as is worth the hearin; I guess you ain't never heerd the morrow [match] of them in your born days. Wal, Bung Swaar, boss, as them Speniards says."

He scratched a match on the side of the door, lit his pipe noisily, and went.

A little way outside the garden gate he stopped and looked back at the house.

"He can keep his blasted old Sunday school," he said, and spat contemptuously.

As he passed the Schoolhouse on his way to Vatster he looked in through the parlour window, the blind of which was hardly ever down, and saw Bob Ertirson and Hakki sitting smoking by the fire.

Bob had been feeling very hopeful all that day, and Magni's joke about the bridegroom in the afternoon had cheered him so much that he had now in the evening come across to Hakki to ask him to give him navigation lessons through the winter. Bob had felt awkward when he first came in; but Hakki had said to him in his usual, immediate style:

"Look here, Bob; I know all about it, and I mean to help dee all I can," and Bob had given Hakki's hand a squeeze that nearly crushed it. His tongue had loosened now he knew that Hakki was his friend, for he felt he could trust him utterly. So they sat speaking about Inga.

They did not know that Erti, with his hot pipe in his waistcoat pocket, had crept up to the window, and now crouched there, listening.

"I think Mann has got some kind of a feeling in that direction," said Hakki, "but it won't do. I don't believe he wants to marry her, and I mean to keep an eye on him. If he's only amusing himself with her, as I suspect, by Heaven, he can look out."

"Yes, he better will," said Bob, and his fist clenched uglily upon his knee.

He turned his face in the direction of the Manse.

"Bit I feel jealous of every sowl in the place sometimes," he added, trying to comfort himself a little with the thought. "Yes, man, sometimes even of a fool laek Erti Gair."

Erti pricked up his ears, and raised his head a bit.

"Yes," said Hakki smiling, "he's about the best specimen of an ass we've got up here. But certainly du needn't let the like of him annoy dee; no lass of any sense would give the fool a look. He's a sly devil though, and good for making any quantity of mischief, if he only has the chance."

Erti raised his head a little more.

Suddenly Bob saw an eye and a small bit of a nose at the left corner of the window. He did not start or give the slightest sign. The eye and nose disappeared, for Erti saw Bob's face towards the window. Then Bob whispered softly,

"Der somebody at da window. Feth, I tink it's Erti Gair."

"Du'll take a cup of coffee with me, Bob," said Hakki in a loud tone. He rose and left the room.

A minute later there was a scuffle outside, for Hakki had slipped round the corner from the kitchen door. When Bob got out, Hakki was holding Erti firmly by the collar.

"Let go, dem it," spluttered Erti, struggling. "I comed in to get a light of this blasted old cutty of mine, as wont go no haow, and I ain't heerd nothin you was a-saying about folks here in the place."

Without further ado Hakki lugged him to the gate, and, with a considerable kick, assisted him on his homeward way.

When he reached Vatster, he found Janny sitting at the fire with a pleased grin upon her "janteel" face. He growled surlily at her till she had spoken to him for a little, and then the grin spread to his "wal-I'm-darned" features also.

Janny had been sitting hatching plans.

Mr. Mann found his mother in the dining-room. She smiled as he came in and said:

"Poor Jacob Bolt seems to take a great interest in you. He was here a little ago, and shook hands with me and said, 'Come moarn, cut coarn'; then he shook hands again and shuffled away."

She did not tell him that Jacob had added:

"Inga boanie lass. Minister laek boanie lass; he, he."

When he had gone upstairs for the night, he went straight to his window and looked across at Taft there in the moonlight. A warm glow came over him as he fixed his eyes on the square, black patch that Inga's window formed in the pale, white light. The night was rather gusty, and the shadows of the big, dark clouds that sometimes hid the moon passed quickly now and then across the land. It seemed to him as if almost everything had grown changeable like that, with big, dark shadows hiding every now and then a light that was no more than pale at best. The sunlight he had seen and felt that summer afternoon three months before when he stood on the top of Da Aest Hill and saw the herring-boat with her brown sail out on the blue sea at the entrance of the voe, had disappeared. The golden sheen that had lain over everything was dimmed. Then, his own lofty aim had lifted him above his people; now, his poor human weakness had set him back again upon their level. His fair dream of hot zeal was over. He blamed himself for instability, for doubt, for want of faith; but that in no way altered the plain fact. He felt there was within him some strange power that was now going blindly on its way in spite of creed or custom, a power he did not understand and therefore could not combat. He knew that he felt jealous of Bob Ertirson, and more to-night than he had ever done before. He thought, with something very much akin to bitterness, of Hakki's words. There was, besides, Aald Erti's criticism of that very morning, and finally that small occurrence in the dusk, with Janny and her possibilities behind it. For the moment he felt that he must now shake himself quite clear of all these things. He had been drifting certainly. Perhaps he was now on his way to being a "sheer hulk," as his late visitor, the "Yenkee," had suggested. But he felt his arms in fancy about Inga still, and this so startled him with its strong vividness that he decided instantly he must give Messrs. Howell and Meek the church and make a big, immediate effort to stir up new interest and life. That would have a tendency to quiet idle tongues. It was, too, on that line of Christian tolerance which he had drawn for himself at the beginning of his ministry.

All at once he noticed that the little window opposite was lighted up. The warm glow rushed over him again. It seemed to him as though some powerful influence were streaming from that window to himself. In imagination he felt

Inga's rounded bosom pressing against his again.

There was lying on his windowsill a big, old telescope, which had formed part of the assets of the late Rev. Mr. Wood, and through which Mr. Mann had often looked for long whiles at a time. It had been wont to lie in the window of the drawing-room, next door to his own room, but for a week or two it had been lying on his bedroom windowsill. His hand touched it now. He took it up. He pulled down the sash and adjusted the glass upon the lighted window.

Inga was in her room. She was feeling her right ankle rather sore, probably, she thought, from having twisted it, when she had slipped down from the steps. She had taken off her shoe and stocking and was looking at it.

Mr. Mann saw a small lamp standing on the little table between the window and the chest of drawers. Then he saw suddenly, full in its light, Inga's white leg, from the rounded knee down to the pretty foot. Once or twice her brow came in sight, as she bent forward.

At that moment Magni Sharp was standing right below Mr. Mann's window, looking up at the end of the spyglass which was dimly visible against the sky. He had felt restless since the instant he had noticed Taft in sight from the chair beside the writing table, and, after his usual crack with the old man in the workshop, he had gone out for a while. He saw the faint glow of the light in Inga's window, the mere top of which appeared above the strip of heather, and he wondered if there was an understanding. Later, as he went slowly up towards Hooll, he heard Bob come out of the Schoolhouse and start west for Sætter. He knew what Bob had been in there about, and he went home, thinking.

After tea next afternoon, Mr. Mann went up to the west "rig," where the folk were busy cutting the corn. He wished to see Jeems Ertirson about the letter.

Jacob was sculling here and there about the field, with his piebald "rivlins," the wisp of straw round his hat, his jacket on the right way now because the days were cooler, and a pleased grin on his features, for he believed that he was looking after everything.

"What's your opinion about it, Jeems?" asked Mr. Mann, when Jeems had read the letter.

"I think ye'll not do it, sir," replied Jeems, slowly, fixing his grave, blue eyes on Mr. Mann's. "We're hed such meetins here i da perrish; bit never i da kirk, an dey're nothin bit excitement an foly. Far be it frae me ta spaek ill o any means of grace, bit I raelly think 'at da good 'at such meetins may do is never sae graet as da evil, for der's a want o all reverence in da wy 'at most o dis waanderin praechers haandles da Wird o God. It's awful ta hear dem sometimes, ignorant men standin dere roarin laek mad folk an coontin demsells fit ta dael wi da mysteries o da kingdom of God. Na, na, sir; it's no laek da praechin ye finn inta da Testament. Wir Saviour wis very calm, an His apostles wis men 'at spak sense an didna just think roarin ta be everything rewhired. Tak ye my advice, sir, an keep on steady wi earnest praechin frae week ta week an God will bliss it in His ain good time, an dat withoot fail."

"Yea, dat He will," fervently assented Oli Jarmson, who was just beside them.

"I understand you, Jeems," said Mr. Mann, flicking the stubble with his stick; "but the excitement that you speak of can be held in check, and the whole movement kept orderly and yet be potent for the good of souls."

"Ye'll excuse me, sir," said Jeems, "bit it's becaase ye're young 'at ye spaek sae. When ye get more experrience o life ye'll come to see 'at howldin things in check is no sae very aesy as ye think at present."

This was the nearest Jeems would come to hinting at the growing frequency of the minister's trips to Taft.

After a little Mr. Mann moved away, with Jacob, who had now come up to him, following closely at his back. The folk were just leaving the field. Aald Erti was by himself setting up the last "stook." He did not hurry from the field as was his wont, for he wished Mr. Mann to see how careful he was about everything connected with the "glibe."

"Well, sir; good evenin, sir," said he, jerkily. "We has had a busy afternoon, as you sees, sir; but 'many hands makes light work,' as the Scripter says, and espeecially when it's the hands of them like myself, for the most part, as has a interest in it, in a menner of speakin, and dont go hurryin from it, as if they didn't care a bug-bu-button, sir,—beg pardon, sir. No, sir, I has a eye to everything, and to show you, sir, as how I takes tally of things, there's fifteen stooks in this race here, sir. I dont say as how I'm perfect in arrametic; but I still knows my simple perdition and superstraction, sir, being quick at figgurs, for the most part, when I was only as high as that nice stick you've got in your hand now, sir."

"Quite so," said Mr. Mann, counting the "stooks" with his eye as he moved away, Jacob following at his heels.

After dark the sky grew thick and rain began to fall. A little after nine o'clock a figure stole out from Vatster and over to the minister's west "rig." It was Aald Erti. He stopped beside the "stook" about which he had spoken to the minister that afternoon. He did not know that Jacob, in his capacity of general manager had been out wandering about the field, had heard him coming, and now lay behind a "stook" quite near, and watched him like a cat.

Aald Erti laid a cow's tether on the ground, took about a dozen sheaves and tied them with it, then got the bundle on his back and started stealthily, not north for Vatster, but up for Da Krö. Jacob moved as stealthily behind him. He saw Erti lay the corn in a corner of the Jarmsons' yard, and then, after glancing carefully about him, make off once more as quietly as possible for Vatster.

When he was fairly gone, Jacob stole out from behind the yard-dyke, and round the corner to the byre door, where he found the cow's tethers hanging hanked. Shortly afterwards he came out from the Jarmsons' yard with the bundle of corn on his back, and a delighted grin upon his face. While Aald Erti sat chuckling by the fire and dried himself, Jacob came softly into the yard at Vatster with his load and hid it in a corner there. Then he came out again, turned round, spat twice, and then set off as fast as he was able home for Taft.

CHAPTER XII

JANNY

"Vitemus oculos hominum, si linguas minus facile possumus."—CICERO

"GOOD mornin, sir," said Aald Erti rather gravely, as Mr. Mann, who, feeling restless, had come out for an early walk, approached him over the stubble of the west "rig," which was now glistening in the morning sunlight after last night's rain.

"Good morning," returned Mr. Mann, wondering a little as he noticed Erti's unusually serious manner.

They were at a little distance from the others, for Erti had shifted from the rest as Mr. Mann came up.

"I am glad, sir," said Erti importantly, "as how you was here on the field yourself last night, sir, and seen the corn. You will recomember as how I told you there was fifteen stooks in this race here, sir, as you seen for yourself, for the most part, as you was a-goin away. Well, sir, when I comes here this mornin the first thing I does, being a man as has had charge of the place afore, sir, is to cast my eye about me, in a menner of speakin, and take tally of everything. And so help me Go-go-goodness, sir,—beg pardon, sir,—I seen at a glance as how there was only thirteen instead of fifteen, and I says to myself, I says, says I, 'Hallo, somebody's been up to somethin here,' says I; for, as you sees, I notices things in a momment, sir, and you can understand the state of concitement it throwed me in, sir, when I tells you that I ain't bitten bread this mornin, sir; no, sir. I says to Janny, sir, I says, says I—---- "

But Mr. Mann thought he saw a discrepancy here.

"Did you know about it before you came to the field?" he asked.

Erti saw that he had stretched out his leg too far; but he was equal to the emergency.

"Lord bless you, sir, beg pardon, sir,—I was out here castin my eye, sir, afore the mornin cup of tea was ready, sir, yes, when you was a-sleepin soundly, sir; it's my naetur, sir, and I can't help it. I feels more careful, yes, of anything as belongs another than I do of my nown, sir; and I dont want to judge my neebur, sir, but you sees for yourself, as how Oli Jarmson hasn't cast his eye over the stooks, sir, and taken tally in a menner of speakin, or he would have knowed as how them two was away, and that's twelve shaefs, sir, or a whole half of a thrave of corn, sir."

"Did you suspect that the corn would be stolen last night?" asked Mr. Mann quietly, fixing his eye on Erti.

"Me, sir? Not me, sir," responded Erti quickly; "but I says to myself when I turns out this mornin, sir, I says, says I, 'I'll perceed to the rig for the more security and see if all be right,' for, as you knows better as me, sir, a open door will temp a saint,' as the Scripter says, which is sound common sense, sir, and no mistake. No, no, sir; I has no wish to bring railin acquisitions, as the Scripter says, against no man, sir; but the corn is gone, and I thinks it nothin but right that all the yards as lie disjacent to the glibe here should be searched at once, sir. I seen things like this happenin afore, sir, both here and when I was out in Whebec, and out there I seen as how they has men as goes about lookin for things, which I disremembers the name for the momment, but thinks as how they calls them defectives, sir. No man as is honest will say nothin again' a fair search as will clear the innicent, and just to show you, sir, I wants you to begin with my yard at Vatster first, sir."

Mr. Mann called to Oli, who came up accompanied by Jacob and listened to the story.

"Weel, sir," said Oli, "we can tak a look ta Vatster, since Erti is sae anxious for it, if ye laek; an efter dat, if ye hae any wish ta dö sae, we can go up ta Da Krö. Bit I tink it'll no be very aesy ta finn da coarn nu, for dem 'at is sae wicked as ta tak what is anidder's is ginerally cute anoff ta laeve few tracks ahint dem, an dey're off wi ean o my tedders too, da vegabonds !"

The three of them at once turned north for Vatster, with Jacob, beaming, at their back.

"He, he," said he, as the procession started, Aald Erti wondering now about that tether.

"I've been a particlar man all my time, sir," said Aald Erti jerkily, "and I knows exackly what corn is in my yard now. There's four screws at the present momment and not another straw, and I is so careful about the fodder, sir, that I takes tally of the day we takes in a screw; yes, I do that in f-f-fack, sir, and just to show you the way I notices, I tells you that the year her that belonged to me wore away, I took in the last screw five days after Candlesmas, sir, on the day after she was entered."

"The day after she was interred," repeated Mr. Mann quietly. "Well?"

"Exackly so, sir," said Erti. "Well, I done the same every year, and I knows to a straw what we has at any momment, sir."

They reached Vatster, and went into the yard.

"Here's the four screws, as you sees, sir," proceeded Erti, leading Mr. Mann and Oli about, while Jacob stood grinning near the gate; "and so help me Go-g-goodness, sir,—beg pardon, sir, as there's not a veesible but them upon the spot of eart', sir."

Then Jacob shuffled in behind the stack in the corner nearest to the gate.

"He, he; twal shaef, Aald Erti tief," he cried in a strident tone.

The three others were approaching the stack. They came round it, and saw the bundle in the corner.

"Well, I'm da-da-daeshed !—beg pardon, sir," said Aald Erti instantly, rising to the occasion, his face darkening with rage. "You sees now the tricks that some of my fine neeburs plays on me."

Aald Erti paused, cleared his throat, and spat.

"Aye, an here's wir tedder," said Oli, examining the rope about the corn.

"Now, look here, men," cried Aald Erti, putting on his most dignified manner, "I dont mind what a poor fool like Jacob here may go and say, because he's luny and can't help hisself, in a menner of speakin; but if any other bug-b-body in this place, sir,—beg pardon, sir,—tries to turn his tongue in his mouth to take away my good name, bi my sowl, I'll have him up at once for definition of character! Yes, I'll go straight off to Lerrick and lay him in!"

Neither Mr. Mann nor Oli could fathom the thing at all, for they saw well enough that Aald Erti would never have been such a fool as to bring them to Vatster in the way that he had done if he had really stolen the corn himself and knew that it was there. But Mr. Mann was angry, and, while Jacob was lifting the bundle of corn on to Oli's back, he turned to Aald Erti and said coldly:

"You need not trouble working any longer on the glebe. Oli will settle with you to-night."

Then he and Oli, with Jacob following, went out of the yard, leaving Aald Erti so enraged that for the moment he said nothing.

When they were gone, however, he spat viciously and muttered through his shut teeth:

"Yes, feth; I wonder who's played me this hell of a trick now; but du can wait dee, Patie Mann, yes, du can wait dee. I'm not done wi dee yet. I'll wind dee a pirm yet."

He stood and watched them till they reached the field. Then he saw Janny, who was working there, leave off and come hurrying north for Vatster.

Jacob did not clear up anything, for he was always most silent when he was most sane.

That evening Janny put the first match to the fuse that she had carefully prepared.

Osla Moar, a woman from a somewhat distant portion of the parish, came along Vatster on her way home from the shop, and Janny made her a strong cup of tea into which she put a drop of spirits, seeing it was Osla. Janny did not hurry. After Osla had drunk the tea, she eructated with considerable force, and said:

"Dat cup o tay is funn my hert."

"Weel, lass; good may it dö dee," said Janny feelingly, "Heard du onything aboot faeder ower at da shop?"

"Yea, lamb," said Osla in a tone that showed she knew how far the machinations of the wicked against honest people sometimes went, "I heard dem spaekin somethin aboot coarn belanging ta da minister 'at wis been fun dis moarnin here ita your yard. It's been da doins o somebody 'at's hed a evil at dy faeder, laekly dem 'at made da lies upon him afore, aboot da glibe. Da place is goin ower wi wickedness an deeviltry."

"Yea, tinks du no?" said Janny. "An da very minister, him 'at oucht ta be reprovin da wicked an no goin aboot tryin ta herm da innicent, is pittin aff his time rinnin efter Inga Bult."

"Na, lass; is yon true?" said Osla eagerly. "I'm heard it turned, wast ower; bit ye canna believe jöst aa 'at ye hear, du kens."

Janny assumed a very righteous air, and leaned nearer to Osla.

"I dont want to make evil upo nonn," she said, in a hoarse whisper, "an du mostna braethe dis til a livin sowl; bit I saa him wi my nown een staandin haddin her in his airms an kissin her, da nicht afore last."

"My gorey, lass," said Osla, perfectly chuckling with delight, "Whar wis yon?"

"I' da public shop," said Janny, tragically.

When Osla was gone, a smile rested on Janny's "janteel" features, as she set up the peats about the fire. She knew that by the time the tale got back from the west side it would have undergone such alterations and repairs as she desired. This was her most artistic style of treatment, which she kept for really juicy bits of news. Little things she flung about quite freely, as the ordinary, small change of gossip; but when she chanced occasionally to get hold of something valuable, she always picked out her first confidante from among such folk as Osla Moar, who lived a good way off, and so the story was quite certain to come home again with suitable additions. She was therefore always careful to select at first a person who had been east at the shop, had come back along Vatster, and was thus outward bound.

About a week after Janny had told Osla, at least a dozen versions of the story had come flying back to Norwik, and Ann Ertirson came hurrying down to Janny with a few of them. This was the cue that Janny had been waiting for. That night, with Aald Erti's strongly oathful approval, she sent Young Erti up to Sætter to see Bob.

When Young Erti got to Sætter he found Bob sitting at the table in the "ben" room, working at his navigation. Bob was quite alone. A lamp was burning on the table, and there was a good fire of blue clods in the grate, which he had put into that room in spite of family objections to the innovation. The warm light was reflected brightly from the brass handles of an old mahogany chest of drawers standing just behind where he was sitting, and from the glass doors of a little bookcase on the top of it, a bit of his own handiwork from the first winter he was home.

Bob had no idea as to what Young Erti could want to see him about. He looked up and bade the "Yenkee" take a chair. Erti, for reasons of his own, selected one at no great distance from the door. Then he stroked his goatee beard as he had done when calling on the minister; but he did not hold his hard felt hat upon his knee, because this night he wore his ordinary clothes and a fur cap that he had brought home from America. His whole bearing showed, however, that he felt this interview to be a much more delicate affair than that had been. He stroked his beard in a way that seemed to hint at a strong sense of duty, coupled with a certain doubt as to the way the other man might look at it. His sly gray eyes kept glancing furtively at Bob, and the "wal, I'm darned" expression on his face had now changed to one of uneasy familiarity.

"Wal, Bob; good evenin," he said, a little quietly for him. "I guess we're in for a spell of bloomin disagreeable weather. Of cowrse I can't say for certain; but thet's my opinion."

"Weel?" said Bob interrogatively.

Erti paused and thought. He had made up his mind to speak about the weather first, and he had done so; but he felt now that he should have started off by speaking to Bob of the navigation he had interrupted.

Bob shoved back his chair, stuck out his legs towards the fire, and kept his eyes on Erti.

"Wal," said Erti carefully, "I guess du's busy with them novigation books."

"No, I'm not," said Bob.

"I guess du was when I comed in," said Erti, trying a small smile.

"Dat's a different thing," said Bob, with a laugh.

"Jest so. I reckon there's a hell of a lot of things in this here world different from what we thinks they is," returned Erti, sententiously, with a slight malicious gleam in his gray eyes.

The words struck Bob unpleasantly, he could not well say why; but he did not catch the gleam of malice in the "Yenkee's" look.

"So, du's noticed dat," said Bob ironically.

"Wal, Bob;" said Erti in a very uneasily familiar tone, but with a touch of what he looked upon as magnanimity, "perheps du thinks as haow I feels a little riled about thet night when Perk comed out and mittened me below thet darned window; but I ain't feelin it worth a cent, because, I seen as haow it was blamed netural for you two fellows to go and suspicion thet I was a-listenin, so I looks over the thing so far and holds as haow you couldn't have done nothin else. I always been freendly to dee; du knows thet."

Erti meant this speech to be a kind of easy introduction to the object of his visit; but he felt he could not quite risk bearing down upon it yet, and so he stopped, cleared his throat impressively, and took another glance at Bob.

"Weel?" said Bob again, looking at him steadily. Erti saw it would be necessary to prepare the way a little more.

He tried a smile again. Then he thought he would feel easier if he smoked. He took his meerschaum, of which he was very proud, from his pocket, and felt in it with his left forefinger.

"Has du got a metch, Bob?" he asked.

"Du'll finn a bit o paper ahint yon chair," said Bob, pointing to it with his foot.

Erti rose, got up the bit of paper, lit his pipe, and took his seat again. Then a bright idea struck him. He would get at the matter through the herring-boat. He cleared his throat again.

"Wal, I guess everything is about right and tight with the 'Inga' naow," he said.

"Yea," said Bob.

Erti paused a moment, then he ventured:

"It's a demd pity every other Inga hedn't got as good a skipper. Thet's what I says."

Bob did not answer; but there was an ominous smile about his lips, the meaning of which the "Yenkee" failed entirely to take in, for he thought this so neat and delicate a bit of flattery that he was sure Bob was quite pleased.

"Yes," he went on with more confidence, "Du knows as haow I've knocked araound a bit, and is in the hebit of goin a thing straight. Wal, I feels it ain't quite on the square for a good man to be put upon by them as hain't no darned right so far, and of cowrse it's netural as haow du shouldn't know about suchlike excep du had a freend as keeps his weather eye open. Naow, what I is a-comin to is this here. Du better skin di eyes, and keep thet minister chep within darned short range. He's hengin raound a certain perty which I dont rewhire to name, excep as haow their initials is 'I. BAY,' and which he ain't got no blamed right to nohaow. Thet perty can't never get no peace for him; but what he's raound there for a constancy, and jest the other evenin he's up, and takes her in his arms, and stands a-kissin of her right in the public sho——!"

Bob rose suddenly. Erti saw by the look on Bob's face that he had better leave as fast as possible. In his fright he dropped his meerschaum on the floor, and the head broke from the stem. Next instant he was in the open air.

Bob took two strides across the floor, picked up the pipe bowl as he passed, and reached the outer door.

Erti's back and quickly moving heels showed for a second in the light streak from the window.

Bob flung the pipe bowl hard, and it hit the "Yenkee" with a crack on the back part of his head; but Bob would not descend to running after him.

When Erti got down to the little bridge across the burn, he knew that Bob had not come after him and he stopped a minute to take breath.

"Blast him," he muttered as he rubbed the back of his head, "I'll be about square with him yet. The fool ain't got no more menners as a grice, or as Megni Sharp."

He smiled at the keenness of his own wit. Then a brilliant notion came into his head.

"Yes," he grinned, "by the Lord Harry, I'll have a shot at I. BAY. slep off naow, and do the beggar out."

When he got to Vatster he dressed himself up carefully in his blue Sunday suit, cursing softly to himself at the sad end of his meerschaum, which would have been, he felt, so useful to him now. Without a word to Janny and Aald Erti, who were anxious for tidings of his trip to Bob, and to their great surprise, he left the house abruptly and hurried east for Taft, as Janny knew by stealing to the corner of the yard to watch the way he took.

Bob turned into his room again and crushed savagely with his heel the stem of Erti's pipe still lying on the floor. He believed the whole thing was a plot of Janny's to torment him, and he felt that Erti's story was a lie. He sat down firmly to his work again. Inga had been particularly pleasant to him all that week, though he had noticed once or twice that she seemed rather nervous, especially when he had spoken to her of his lessons. But soon he could not work. What if this thing were true? He felt inclined to call in Ann and ask her if she had heard anything; but he shrank from this, and sat staring at the fire instead.

As Erti passed the parlour window east at Taft, he saw Inga in the room alone. He stepped to the porch door and knocked. Inga rose somewhat hurriedly and came to open it, for she half thought the knock was Mr. Mann's.

"Good evenin," said Erti in his best form, and holding out his hand, which Inga took with a puzzled, half-contemptuous air. "You is the very perty as I wants to see, if so be it's quite agreeble naow."

Inga felt tempted to slam the door in his face at this, for his conceit made her so angry; but she felt curious to know what he could want with her, and so she said:

"Come in through."

"Wal," said the "Yenkee" as he took a chair beside the fire and stroked his goatee beard with one hand, while his other held his hat upon his knee, "I been thinkin of droppin in, like, some evenin and seein you about a certain metter, as is between ourselves like."

"Yes?" said Inga questioningly, as she sat down on a chair out at the corner of the table.

"Jest so," said Erti, with a smile, as if he knew quite well the proper quantity of introduction to be used in such a case as this at any rate. "You knows as haow I've knocked araound a bit and seen the world, and ain't just layed up here like a bloomin peat all my time, as some young fellows as we knows of done. When I was in the States, I seen me earn as high as ten dollars a day sometimes. Wal, I got a little money laid by."

He had thirteen shillings in a tobaccobox in the locker of his trunk.

"Yes, I often thinks of goin away to the States again, and you bet, thet's the place where women is treated like leddies, and ain't got to carry muck and suchlike, but sits on a fine sofa all day, and amuses theirselves like. I guess the likes of you is just about sick of this old place sometimes, for it ain't fit for a beauty like you nohaow."

He paused to give this time to dry.

Inga gave a wicked little smile and said,

"Yes, it truly is dull here at times."

"I reckon you'd feel happy all the bloomin time, if you was wance out in the States."

"But wha have I to tak me there?" said Inga with a mischievous look upon her face.

Erti thought a golden moment had arrived. He rose and stepped towards where Inga sat. She saw what he was after, and she jumped up to get away from him. But the chair was in her way, and, as she stumbled and could not box his ears, he tried to put his arm round her neck. His face was towards the window.

Suddenly, against the darkness, he saw Bob's face looking in. He was about to make a tender speech; but he said instead, as he snatched his arm away,

"I guess I wont fash you any longer to-night. Evenin!"

He bolted out at the kitchen door, as Bob stepped quickly into the front porch.

CHAPTER XIII

MARY

"Wir glauben all' an einem Gott."—LUTHER

MR. and Mrs. Mann and Hakki had been asked to come and spend that evening at the Ha. Mr. and Mrs. Mann had gone, and Hakki had sent word that he would come down about eight, when he was through with Bob.

As Mr. and Mrs. Mann walked south along the shore, his thoughts were full of Inga. Since that night of the telescope, he had been only once at Taft, and he and Inga both had blushed on meeting for the first time after the shop steps. He had wondered a little at her blush, for she had seemed so cool in Janny's presence and even after she was gone; but her blush pleased him, though it startled him as well. He had been daily expecting to hear Janny's version of the fall in circulation, and he had sometimes stopped upon his way upstairs to listen to stray sentences that floated from the kitchen.

As he neared the Ha, he felt his mind shift round, he knew not why, to Mary Black. He wondered at this strange tendency to think of girls, that had grown up so quickly in him. No warm glow passed over him at the thought of Mary Black; but he was conscious of a quiet sense of pleasure, an anticipation of sweet mental sympathy and coy companionship, through which shot piquant gleams and flashes of a character unusually developed for her years.

She met them at the garden gate. Mrs. Black was at the door, and she took Mrs. Mann at once into the house, leaving him and Mary in the garden by themselves.

The night was fine. The air was still and not particularly chilly. There was no sound but now and then the barking of a dog from one or other of the crofts, and the slow wash of the sea upon the shore below. As he stood beside her there inside the garden gate, upon the path, he felt as if some new and subtle influence from her touched him. He was quite near her. The wide sleeve of her silk blouse rustled on his sleeve, as he turned half round and said:

"Shall we go up by the other path?"

"Yes, if you like," she answered, and they moved along the path that passed the little arbour in the corner. The delicate fragrance of the white rose perfume which she used, came faintly to him. He wondered whether she had heard much of the gossip about his late trips to Taft.

"Mamma was telling me that two of those itinerant preachers have written to you asking for the church. I hope you will not think of giving it," she said in her outspoken way.

"Well, really, I have not yet settled as to that," he answered, feeling, as he had often felt with her, that she went right into a matter, as if there was bound to be a free exchange of sentiments between them.

"You should settle to refuse," she said decidedly. "You will only disarrange your work, and hurt yourself if you bring men like that into the place. I don't think you have been quite careful enough already."

"In what way?" he asked, a little hesitatingly.

"You know what I mean," she answered, in her quiet, clear, voice, "it would have been better for you if you had had a sister. Your mother is too gentle. I think she is afraid of you."

"I have often wished that I had had a sister," he said slowly, wondering at this new tone she had suddenly assumed. "Will you not take the place of one to me?"

She gave a little laugh.

"I am going to do that," she said, "and you must listen to me when I speak to you. You have just come from your study where the light is dim, and there are many things you do not see quite clearly yet, many things that a girl can see quite clearly. You must not go to Taft so often."

He scarcely knew what to say, and he was glad that it was dark. They were just opposite the corner in which were the elder bushes and the garden seats.

"Shall we sit down here for a few minutes?" he said quickly, for he did not want to go into the light just then.

"Yes; but only for a very few," she answered with another little laugh.

He pushed aside the branches for her, and as she brushed past him he was conscious of a thrill of pleasure at her nearness to him. There was something in it similar to and something different from the way he felt in Inga's presence. They sat down on the nearer seat.

"You must pull yourself together," she went on. "You have been letting yourself drift. I said to you the first day that we saw each other that I believed you were trying too much, and I was surer of it afterwards. But you would not come here much, and so I did not get a chance to tell you what I thought. You have given us nothing but short visits now for weeks. Some evenings when we asked you, I think you went to Taft instead. I know quite well how it may look to you for me to speak like this; but I have inherited directness as you see and if you do not understand me, you have much less mind than I have thought. Inga is a pretty girl, and a nice girl too, and she has got some education. I do not wonder that you have felt drawn to her; but you should not let yourself drift in the way that you are doing. You do not understand yourself, for you are but a boy in things like these. Do you mean to marry her?"

The question made him start. He had never thought of that as anything but a remote contingency.

"You speak very plainly," he said awkwardly, and he felt the warm blood mount to his face.

"You wished me to become your sister," she said quietly.

Her honesty towards him struck him forcibly.

They both sat silent for a while.

Hakki waited half-an-hour, then, feeling sure that something had kept Bob from coming, he decided to start for the Ha. He had opened the front door when he remembered he had left his pipe upon his bedroom mantelpiece. He shut the door and turned back into the bedroom, which was just across the lobby from the parlour. From the kitchen it was easy to imagine that he had gone out. He heard someone go quickly into the parlour, and he watched to see this person coming out again. From the dark bedroom he saw in the parlour doorway against the firelight the plump figure of Lowra Sharp. She was carrying some books in her hand. Once or twice lately he had noticed that his books had been disturbed, and now he knew the reason. He went out quietly, thinking about this.

When he got down to the Ha and was walking along on the soft grass by the garden wall, he all at once heard voices, and he stopped.

"You are more than a sister now," said Mr. Mann, and Hakki smiled.

"He's a rare boy, this Peter," said he to himself.

"I hope to be more to you still," said Miss Black quietly, "since I see that you understand and trust me. But we must really go in now."

"Ho, ho," said Hakki to himself.

At supper, Hakki thought the minister a good deal brighter than was usual with him, and he watched him closely.

"You'll take a glass of wine with me this evening, Mr. Mann," said Mr. Black, good-humouredly. "I believe in temperance myself, but this total abstinence of yours is nothing but a fad, and quite unscriptural, you know. You'll take a glass of claret. It's not much stronger than our national beverage of 'blaand.'"

"Which is only milk and water," answered Mr. Mann with a smile. "That is not very deadly. I am by no means, Mr. Black, a rabid abstainer, as you seem to suppose; but I hold it is best to be extremely moderate and careful in the use of all such beverages. This evening I will take a glass of claret with you."

Mrs. Mann turned pale. Mary looked hard at him; but he was looking at the laird.

"Yes, that is the strongest way," said Mrs. Black warmly. "It is only very weak people who are afraid to use the good creatures of God, in case they may abuse them."

"Many people are much weaker than they think themselves," said Mary sharply.

"Certainly, my dear," said Mrs. Black, with a smile. "It's a great pity, but there are so many people who cannot distinguish between those who use stimulants as beverages and those who use them as medicines."

"A prescription might assist to clear a point like that," said Hakki in his usual vein.

"A proscription in some cases might be preferable," said Mr. Black, to whom Hakki's presence was a fillip always, pouring out the wine for Mr. Mann.

"Have you heard of the projected visit of those howling dervishes in December, Mr. Black?" asked Hakki, with a glance at Mrs. Mann.

"O, yes," answered Black; "but I do not know whether Mr. Mann has yet decided to inflict them on the parish then or not. What are you going to do, Mr. Mann?"

Mann glanced at Mary. She was looking at him still. He took a sip of his claret, and said a little hurriedly:

"Mr. Bolt thinks I should let them have the church."

"Yes; Uncle likes to bring the folk about the shop," said Hakki, with a bit of ham upon his fork.

"I do not think you are quite fair to Mr. Bolt," returned Mann, looking across at Hakki, while his tone showed that he felt inclined to-night to pick up any gauntlet Hakki might throw down.

"I am fairer to him than he is to himself," said Hakki with a smile. "He generally succeeds in letting the balance swing to his own side."

"You will admit, I think, that he has also some small interest in the spiritual progress of the people," said Mann with a touch of sarcasm, which Mary noted with a certain pleasure, since it was being used to quiet Hakki.

"Certainly," returned Hakki heartily. "That's just what I am explaining to you. He has the keenest interest in the spiritual progress of the people, whenever such progress can occur in the vicinity of Taft."

Black saw quite clearly from the tone the two men had assumed that both were eager for a fight of wits.

"The spiritual progress of the people is an interesting topic," he said with a laugh, "and we must thrash it out in my room after supper, and so avoid boring the ladies with polemics."

"The discussion would not bore us, pa," said Mary eagerly, for though she disliked Hakki, she was anxious to see a mental fight between him and Mann, who would, she felt sure, hold his own if he was once aroused.

"You should say 'me,' not 'us,' my dear," interposed Mrs. Black with a dissatisfied air. "All those disputes are very stupid, I think, and unbecoming. Don't you think so, Mrs. Mann?"

"Except where they are absolutely necessary," answered Mrs. Mann gently, but with something of firmness in her tone as well, for she was sitting bracing herself up to speak to Peter afterwards about that glass of claret, and the fear that she might rouse the fiend of temper that she knew slept in him tortured her.

"I think they are always necessary," said Mary enthusiastically, "for they wake up the mind and prevent it from sitting dozing over things that have become familiar to it in one form only."

Mann wondered if she meant this speech for him. He saw her glance at him, and then at Hakki and her father. She looked very pretty in her eagerness, and the keenness of her mental view delighted him. He wished they had stopped longer in the garden, and he felt that he would rather stay and talk to her than go with Hakki to Black's room as soon as they had finished supper, to sit and smoke and argue.

"But Mr. Mann has not yet told us what he means to do about those dervishes," resumed the laird.

"I think I shall let them have the church," said Mann a little nervously, for the thought of Janny Gair was in his mind.

He glanced at Mary again, and saw that she looked disappointed. He did not meet her look.

"I think it is our duty to use every means of grace," said Mrs. Mann earnestly. She thought of that revival meeting years before, where Peter's father had heard that which turned him from drink and from much else, although it did not while he lived cast out the devil of his temper.

Then the conversation wandered all about the parish, and beyond it. Half an hour later, Mrs. Black rose, and said:

"We must send the gentlemen away now to their smoking and their squabbling."

"That was a curious thing about your corn last week, Mr. Mann," remarked the laird as the three men gathered round the fire in his own sanctum, "I can't see what motive that silly old fellow Erti Gair could have had in getting you and your man to come right over to Vatster to find the stolen sheaves in his own yard."

"I have no idea as to what he meant," said Mann slowly. "It is quite inexplicable, for he is so very sly. From what you told me, his former connection with the glebe was not much to the advantage of Mr. Wood."

"Sly is a euphemism for his character," said the laird with a laugh. "He's an unprincipled rascal, like a good few others of his class. Wait till you have lived here as long as I have and then you'll know to what extent dishonesty and laziness prevail. That old scoundrel is a type."

"He is a product also, to a great extent," said Hakki, rapidly lighting his pipe. "He is in part the answer to the problem which your ancestors worked out."

Black smiled.

"How so?" he asked.

"Well," said Hakki incisively, "your ancestors robbed and oppressed his ancestors and mine in every conceivable way; destroyed their free institutions, their law courts, their land-tenure, their rights and liberties as men; swindled them with false weights and measures, the apparatus of iniquitous extortion; stole their lands, their sheep, their cattle, their household goods, their daughters, their honour, and their freedom—made them slaves, in short; crushed the life and spirit out of them with the iron heel of Scotch brutality and greed, because they were not numerous enough to offer adequate resistance. What weapon was left to them but deceit? What defence had they but to meet fraud with fraud? Those of them who could, fled back to Norway; but the bulk of them were forced to stay and sink down into an abyss of misery. What do you think you would have been like yourself, my friend, you, Robert Black, Esq., if your ancestors had been ground for some centuries in such a mill of hell?"

"Probably a crofter," returned Black, with another smile. "Yes, that's a heavy indictment you bring against us; but what have I to do with those oppressions? I have frequently been swindled and oppressed myself by the numerous class of characters like this old Erti."

Hakki laughed.

"Don't you see that they were simply balancing accounts?" he said. "It's always class that squares accounts with class. That's how God works out the permutations and combinations of history. It is inconvenient when the answer takes a long time to come and then comes all at once, as in the French Revolution. With a small handful of people the turn of the poor never comes. You are a type and a product as well as Aald Erti. It is strictly scriptural if you suffer sometimes. Mr. Mann will tell you about the third and fourth generations, etcetera."

Mann sat looking sharply at him. His feeling towards him had grown bitterer steadily since that day of the violent hint. Now that the three of them were by themselves he momentarily feared Perk would make some allusion of a pungent nature to the little scene at Taft, of which he must have heard; but Perk's invariably sarcastic manner angered him, and he determined to return his shot.

"And so you would condone dishonesty?" said Mann severely.

"I did not give you credit for being so obtuse," replied Perk with a smile. "I do not defend dishonesty; I simply call attention to one of its roots. Its eradication is part of my daily work, a part of work that the old, soul-saving machine of which you are an engineer seems quite unable to accomplish. I maintain that long-continued oppression and injustice form one chief cause of the dishonesty and laziness of which Mr. Black complains, and of which you have got a taste yourself in this case of Aald Erti."

"Yes; but wait a moment, Mr. Perk," said Black. "What about the conduct of these same Norse ancestors of yours before? Did they not oppress, or rather exterminate the Picts, or whatever other people they found here when they came? Perhaps Providence sent my ancestors as the avengers of those slaughtered Picts."

Hakki laughed.

"That explains the first stage, we'll say," he said; "but what about that iron heel of Scotch greed sticking there for centuries? Providence, it seems, forgot to call off His dogs again."

"You seem to regard the mere holding of land as oppression," said Mann pointedly.

"Yes, in certain circumstances," returned Hakki. "Suppose we say my ancestors and Mr. Black's were robbers, it's a pity that the plunder is not better parted among their posterity. The Church was as great a robber as the rest. I don't expect Mr. Black and you to sell all you have and give it to the poor, for you believe that to be nonsense, although you are afraid to say so from the pulpit. In the old Norse days, men would have put right some of these things with a bit of steel."

"And put as many others wrong," Mann added. "We live under a better Dispensation, God be thanked."

"Are the climate and the soil of the islands any better under your Gospel than they were when people worshipped Thor and Odin? The land tenure is certainly much worse," said Hakki with a laugh.

"The Gospel has quieted men's lives," replied Mann earnestly; "brought civilisation in its train, with such arts and inventions, trade and intercourse, as make men independent of both soil and climate."

"But not yet of landlords," added Perk.

"You can't dispute the effect that Christianity has had upon society," persisted Mann.

"Yes, its morals; not its dogmas," said Hakki smiling. "Aald Erti there, accepts your dogmas; and dispenses with your morals. Had you not better preach plain honesty for a while, and strict temperance in regard to feminine society?"

Mann winced.

But just then a knock came to the door. It was Jeanie Ertirson to say that Betty Jeemson from Taft was wanting to see Mr. Perk.

Hakki left the room and went to Betty at the kitchen door.

"What's up?" he asked.

"Dey're wantin you ta come ower ta Taft at wance," said Betty rapidly, "for somethin is happened."

CHAPTER XIV

HEARTS

"Imellem kan tankerne listende fare."—BJÖRNSON

INGA heard the footsteps in the porch. This time she thought it must be Mr. Mann, and she smiled to herself, though she was in a temper at Young Erti's impudence. She stepped quickly to the parlour door, and came face to face with Bob. He was very plainly angry.

"What did dat fool want here?" he asked roughly, pushing past her into the room.

She did not answer him, but went and sat down on the same chair as before, and he stood on the hearthrug, looking at her.

"What did dat fool want here?" he repeated almost harshly, for his suspicion and jealousy had been growing in him all the way east from Sætter.

She looked up at him sharply.

"What business is it o dine?" she asked, with temper in her tone.

After her late kindliness, this tone was torture to him. He felt it would be best to calm himself if possible, as he usually tried to do whenever she got angry. But it seemed to him that it was simply cruel of her to use that tone to him, because she knew quite well that it was love of her that made him speak so roughly. He was smarting under that sight of Erti's impudence which he had witnessed through the window; but the thought of Erti's story about Mr. Mann was worse, and he believed it now.

His question about Erti was actually a question about Mann.

"I understaand dee," he said in a choked voice. "Yes, this is a more sensible place than the public shop; but it's a pity du wisna carefuller aboot the man."

He felt this to be contemptible when he had said it, for he had seen quite well what was the real state of things when he looked through the window; but he had lost his self-control.

"What does du mean?" asked Inga, with an angry flash in her blue eyes.

"I mean simply this," he answered passionately, his hands clenched by his sides. "For three years du never gae me encouragement by word or look; but I waited lovin dee an hopin, becaase it was the same as life an death to me. Three months ago I thought I saw a change; but it seems I was a fool to think it. Du knows as weel as me what grounds I had for thinkin it. Du would have done a kinder thing if du had left me as I was afore. What need had du to decaeve me? I never tried to hurt dee in my life. God knows, no man could love dee better as I've done an do."

His vehemence surprised and frightened her. She saw the false position in which first her vanity and then her weakness had now placed her, and for the moment she despised herself and pitied Bob with all her heart. She felt she must be honest with him now.

"Look here, Bob," she said, plucking at the tablecloth and trying to steady her voice, but avoiding his look, "I know I've done wrong to dee, an I'm truly sorry for it."

He thought she was going to explain all and relieve his pain, and his face cleared for a moment.

"Du's always been good to me," she went on hesitatingly, "an gentle wi me in spite o all my nonsense, an I know I never had a truer friend. But, Bob, I canna help it. I dont feel that I want dee to be more."

His face darkened again. But she did not still look up.

"I suppose that's what du meant all the time," he said with a bitter sneer, which came so strangely from him that she felt her heart beat violently with fear.

"O, Bob, dont," she said pleadingly, and, glanced up at him. She saw his face was hard and set.

"Efter the past three months, an more especially efter last week I think du might at anyrate say why du feels like that," he said in a keen, cold tone, that made her tremble. "Does du love another man?"

She wondered whether she should fling herself upon his mercy, and try to keep his friendship and remove his anger by a confidence. From his tone, she feared it was too late.

"Bob," she said, and she rose from the chair and came over to him, "dont be like yon to me. Truly I canna help it."

The words touched him for an instant; but as he looked at her standing there beside him, her face flushed, her bosom heaving, every charm that had attracted him heightened by her agitation, his old, wild longing seized him, and he felt that he could kill the man that came between them.

"Does du love another man?" he asked again, and the words came harshly from his throat.

She felt that confidence was useless now. His harshness hurt her. She did not think her conduct to him had given him the right to treat her so. Her temper rose suddenly again.

"What if I do?" she said cuttingly.

He turned half round from her, then turned back again.

"I understaand," he burst out fiercely, for the thought that Mann had had her in his arms maddened him. "Yes, it's that sneakin, white-faced devil Mann I have to thank for this. God pity him, if I get my hands on him this night."

The agony of his hopeless love had mastered him. He shook with rage. His eyes were burning in his head.

He turned from her suddenly again.

"Bob," she cried, and caught him by the arm; but he pulled his arm from her, and, with a curse, strode from the room.

She did not spring after him; but stood listening to his angry footsteps. She saw the light gleam on his face as he went past the window. Then she sat down on the bulky haircloth sofa, and put her hand against her side.

She scarcely knew what to do. She was terrified at the thought of what might happen. In a little while however, she felt somewhat better, for she felt that Bob's usual moderation would assert itself; but this was only for a moment, for she knew that she had never seen him act before as he had done that night. She turned pale at the thought of his slow anger now at last aroused. After about ten minutes she rose and ran into the shop, where her father and mother were.

"Is Bob been here?" she asked excitedly.

"No," answered Hansi, and she turned to the door again and looked out into the darkness. Then she came back.

"Is Mester Mann?" she asked, and this time more excitedly.

"No," answered Hansi once more, without looking up from the desk, where he sat writing letters.

"What is it, Inga?" asked Willa, looking at her curiously.

"It's nothin," she answered with a laugh that was nearly a sob. Then she ran out again. She went to the south end of the house and stood there listening; but she heard no sound, except the barking of a dog at Hooll. She hurried back into the parlour and through it to the kitchen.

"Is onybody been in?" she asked Betty, who was getting ready supper.

"Young Erti Gair gaed oot a while ago," returned Betty with a smile. "I'm seen non else."

Jacob was sitting dozing in his big chair by the fire. He suddenly sat up and looked at Inga.

"He, he," he chuckled. "Twal shaef; Aald Erti tief."

She went back to the parlour, and a little later to the shop again. She hurried three or four times between the shop and the house, and every time she did so she ran to the south end of the house and listened.

The last time she did this she heard heavy footsteps coming round the corner of the yard.

"Is it dee, Bob?" she cried; but Magni Sharp's voice answered her.

"Na," said Magni, coming quickly to her side, "it's me. Is Bob no here?"

That day Magni had been at the westside, and on his way home in the evening he dropped in at Sætter to see Bob. But Bob had gone out, and his folk did not know where he was. They did not think he had gone to the Schoolhouse, for he had left his books. Magni sat for a few minutes, and then went again. When he had crossed the burn and got a little east of Vatster, he heard a man coming rapidly towards him. The man was quite close before he recognised him as Young Erti in his Sunday clothes.

"Wal, Megni," said the "Yenkee," stopping, and doing all he could to keep an easy air, "I guess there's a hell of a shindy on naow, down there at Taft. I reckon Bob's heerd as haow Mann was a-kissin of I. BAY. thet night, for him and her was givin each other a almighty tearin up, when I comed pest the window of the perlour not long sin syne."

Then Magni had come hurrying east to Taft.

"O, Magni, I'm blide du's come," said Inga in an excited whisper, and she seized his arm.

His long repressed devotion to her swelled up in him at her touch. He put his arm tenderly about her shoulders, for he felt that she was trembling. But he had given himself to Bob and to her, utterly. She knew what he was feeling, and a great pity for him stirred her.

"Yes; he's been here," she faltered, "and he's gone awey in a passion. O, Magni, dont lat him touch the minister."

"Geng du in, Inga," he said gently. "I'll geng efter him."

He turned and walked rapidly away.

She listened to his strong, quick footsteps for a little, then she ran into the house.

Hansi and Willa shut the shop, and came in to supper. Inga sat down at the table with them; but she did not eat.

All at once she gave a scream, and slipped, fainting, from her chair, upon the floor.

Hansi sprang to her, and, lifting her in his strong arms, laid her on the sofa. Willa echoed her scream, and, springing to her, knelt beside her.

Her face was white. Her eyes were closed. After a few minutes she opened them and looked right at her father.

"Tell Hakki to come here," she whispered, closing them again. It seemed as if she thought that Hakki was then in the house.

Hansi hurried to the kitchen, and bade Betty run and fetch him.

Betty ran up to the Schoolhouse. She found her aunt Kirsty in the kitchen, with Lowra Sharp sitting beside her, reading. They told her Hakki had gone to the Ha. She said that Inga had turned ill, and wanted Hakki instantly; and she ran on to the Ha.

As Hakki, hurrying north to Taft with Betty, passed the Manse, he heard voices at the corner of the garden; but he did not stop.

Inga was lying with her eyes closed when he entered.

She heard him coming in, and slightly raised herself.

"Geng but, faeder, an tak midder wi you," she said in a low voice, and the old folk went into the kitchen, leaving her and Hakki by themselves.

"What's wrong, Inga?" asked Hakki anxiously.

He had stepped to the sofa and was bending over her.

She suddenly flung her arms about his neck, and, pulling his head down upon her breast, began to sob.

"Dunna be hard on me, Hakki," she whispered brokenly. "I have none but dee."

For the moment he did not understand her.

"O, Hakki," she went on, "I wish I had done what du bade me, an tald Bob plainly afore; but truly I was frightened, an nu when I tried ta tell him he's gone oot in a passion ta seek Mester Mann, for somebody is gone an tald him lies aboot yon night when I fell i da shop." Then the terrible earnestness of Bob's love stood out for an instant in her mind in contrast to Mann's hesitating manner to her and his fear of Janny Gair.

There came to Hakki a remembrance of the time when they were children. He felt he had been rather hard with her, and he was sorry now. He raised himself and took her hand in his.

"Look here, Inga," he said with unusual gentleness, "I want dee to tell me everything. Is there anything between dee and Mann? Has he said anything to dee?"

Her face flushed.

"No, he's never said anything," she answered.

"Does du care for him diself?" he asked.

"Yes," she almost whispered. "I canna help it, Hakki."

The fact that she had now returned to her old openheartedness with him affected him. He felt he could not urge Bob's suit, as he had promised, now. The only thing he could do was to calm her, and calm Bob, if possible, and wait a bit. He was surprised to find himself with such a mild view of the case. But his resentment against Mann sprang up again. He despised him for his weakness. He felt that it would serve him right if Bob went and explained things forcibly to him that night. Then he thought of Mann's mother and of Inga and the little world about them. Inga seemed to read his thoughts.

"Magni was here, an he said he wid go efter him; but der non sae strong as dee Hakki. O, will du go an spaek ta Bob?" she said, her hand twitching nervously in his.

He suddenly bent down and kissed her on the lips. She flung her arms about his neck again and held him for a moment, and for that moment Hakki hesitated. He knew he could not now help Bob with her, and a fierce jealousy of Mann rose in him. Why should he not, at least, take her from Mann.

Just then, Lowra Sharp, who had come hurrying from the Schoolhouse, passed the parlour window and looked in at them, then started and turned pale.

"Yes, I'll go, Inga," said Hakki quietly, raising himself. He stepped quickly to the door. At the porch door he met Lowra.

"Whar's Inga?" she asked in a strained voice.

"Go in, Lowra," he said abruptly, and passed out.

The quiet of the night was gone. The wind had all at once begun to puff up from the north, and the air had turned cold. He hurried south towards the Manse. At the corner of the garden wall he heard the voices he had heard before, and one of them was loud and angry. The angry voice was Magni's. Bob was speaking quietly; but his voice was hard.

As he reached them, he heard Mr. and Mrs. Mann coming round the south corner of the garden wall. She was coughing, and he was speaking to her.

Bob and Magni stood silent.

Mr. and Mrs. Mann approached the gate in the middle of the wall. Bob made a movement to step round the corner, and Hakki seized his arm. Bob shook him off.

CHAPTER XV

TWO SCENES

"And nothing can we call our own but death."—SHAKESPEARE

HAKKI seized Bob's arm again. Magni seized the other. He felt that he would rather knock Bob down than let him go loose in his passion. Bob stood still. He had meant to go first quietly up to Mann and ask him to come out and speak to him after he had taken his mother into the house.

"I thought I heard someone at the corner of the garden," said Mr. Mann as they reached the gate.

"It must have been some people passing," said Mrs. Mann; but he felt suspicious.

Bob made another movement. The others held him.

"Du'll lose her forever, if du stirs," whispered Hakki in his ear, and the words startled him.

Mr. and Mrs. Mann went in.

"Come home wi me, Bob," said Hakki in a clear, hard tone. "It's dy last chance." Magni let go Bob's arm. For a little Bob stood still, trying to master himself, then he slowly turned, and the three started for the Schoolhouse. When they reached the gate, Magni turned north to Hooll, for he thought it better to leave Bob to Hakki.

When Mrs. Mann had gone upstairs, Mann went into the kitchen.

"Did you hear any noise outside here a little ago, Naanie?" he asked. She went and shut the kitchen door before she answered him.

"Yes," she said, looking intently at him, "an I ran oot an listened. It was Bob Ertirson an Magni Sharp, an dey wir spaekin aboot Inga."

"Do you know what is the matter?" he asked nervously. "I heard at the Ha that Miss Bolt had suddenly taken ill. Betty came there, running, to fetch Mr. Perk. I must step over to Taft and enquire."

"You can do dat i da mornin," said Naanie meaningly. He did not answer her; but opened the kitchen door and went out.

As he passed the parlour window at Taft, Inga heard and knew the footsteps that she had been sitting straining her ears to catch. She was sitting on the sofa, with Lowra on a chair beside her.

"Wait dee, Lowra," she said excitedly. "It's Mester Mann." She sprang up and ran from the room, closing the door behind her. She opened the porch door before he knocked.

"Come in," she said in a faint voice; but he knew her. He stepped in, and she quickly closed the door.

"Come upstairs," she whispered, and he checked the anxious question that was on his lips and followed her, a strange sensation passing over him. They went up into the "best-room," which was above the shop. She took his hand to guide him in the dark, pulled him gently into the room and closed the door. He kept hold of her hand when she tried to withdraw it.

"I heard you had turned ill suddenly," he said anxiously. She did not answer, but began to sob. He drew her closer to him. She made no resistance.

"What's the matter, Miss Bolt—Inga?" he asked in a low, eager tone. She pressed close up to him, but did not answer still. He felt her right breast touch him. They were just beside the sofa. He slipped his arm about her and drew her down upon it.

"What's the matter, Inga?" he asked tenderly again; but she clung to him without speaking. The same strong longing he had had when he had caught her falling from the steps came on him now. This time he did not try to conquer it. He clasped her wildly to him, and, for a while, sat silent, drunk with the delight of her embrace. He pressed his lips upon her brow. She raised her face. He felt her bosom heaving against his, and he sank his burning lips on hers. In that hot kiss he thought of her, and her alone, and, swept away by a great wave of passion, he murmured in her ear:

"I love you, Inga."

She leaned against his breast without moving. Her sobbing ceased. Then she whispered brokenly:

"Bob was here to-night." The words roused him.

"But you have never encouraged him," he whispered passionately. He felt her shiver slightly; but she did not answer, and a cold breath of fear passed over him, to be followed instantly by a new wave of longing.

"You love me, Inga?" he said with desperate earnestness, and he pressed hot lips on hers again.

"Yes," she whispered faintly, when her lips were free.

They both sat silent for a little time. Then she said softly:

"Somebody has told him about that night in the shop."

The words jarred painfully on him. Why was she harping on Bob like this? A jealous anger seized him.

"What has he to do with that?" he asked sharply. "You have never encouraged him?"

She did not know what to say.

"No" was on her lips, but her conscience pricked her.

She seemed to droop in his arms.

"Are you ill, Inga?" he asked with quick anxiety.

"Yes," she answered faintly; "but you must go now, and come back to-morrow." She pulled herself up by her arms, which were about his neck. The action fanned the flame in him again.

When he got out in the cold north wind, he wondered whether he were mad. The blood was dancing wildly in his veins. He felt that he must go to Taft to-morrow—yes, every day. He was seized with the idea that he must run and leap; but he checked this, and walked quickly south towards the Manse. As he crossed the strip of heather, he looked west and saw a light gleaming from the Ertirsons' window at Sætter. A feeling of elation that was almost cruel came over him.

He saw a light, too, in the Schoolhouse, and caught a glimpse of two dark figures in the lighted doorway, which closed just as he looked. As soon as he came in, Naanie told him that his mother wished to speak to him before he went to bed, and he went right up to her room. He was distinctly conscious of a strangely deepened thrill of filial love.

"Peter," said Mrs. Mann tremulously, putting out her hand to him, when he had sat down by the bed, "you know what we both suffered in the old, dark days. O, Peter, promise me that you will never take a glass of wine or any kind of strong drink again. I cannot bear it. I have feared to speak to you, for I know you have your father's temper; but it is to save you, Peter."

"O, mother," he said, and in his excited state of feeling tears came into his eyes. "How could you fear me? Yes, I promise you never to taste drink again. It has no hold on me whatever, and I do not fear for myself in the least; but for your sake I will leave it quite alone."

"Kiss me, Peter," she murmured, and he bent to her. Now that she thought the biggest danger of his life was past, she smiled and grew quite playful, saying to him:

"Don't you think Miss Black a very pretty girl, and so bright and clever?"

He did not answer, but she saw his face was flushed.

"I understand, Peter," she said, with a quiet, little laugh, and gently pressing his hand. "You needn't mind my knowing, and it makes me feel so glad. Now, run off to bed like a good boy. Good-night."

In his own room he stood for a long while with his face towards Taft. He said to himself that he would not go to the Ha now except in the most cursory way. His whole mind was filled with the thought of Inga, and waves of love and jealousy swept one upon the other over him. He did not fall asleep till four o'clock.

When Bob left the Schoolhouse he was actually a good deal calmed; but he felt strongly tempted, as Hakki closed the door, to turn back to the Manse and try to see Mann now, when there was no one to come in the way. He had said, however, that he would go home, and he was going, doggedly. As he passed the corner of the dyke, someone sprang up suddenly from behind it and ran off in the darkness. It was Young Erti. He had changed back to his wearing clothes and come out to get news of Bob. He had been watching Bob and Hakki through the window; but, acting on his former experience of this, he had subsequently withdrawn to the corner of the dyke. Bob had come so close that he thought Bob had seen him.

Bob set off after him. He guessed it was Young Erti, but they had got down close to the burn at the foot of the Vatster "rigs" before he was quite certain. There he overtook him. He seized him by the neck and sent him on his stomach in the mud, tripped over his heels, and landed on the top of him. Neither of them spoke. In a few minutes Bob had got a black eye and Erti a severe pounding. When Bob thought that he had given him enough, he took him, kicking and hitting out, by the neck and the rear of his trousers, and, after giving him a savage shake, flung him into the burn. Then he went on doggedly up to Sætter.

Erti crawled out, dripping and blaspheming breathlessly, and stumbled north for Vatster.

"My Lord, boy, whar's du been?" cried Janny as he entered. He answered her with an oath. Aald Erti said nothing, for he was wiser. Two nights later the "Yenkee" donned his Sunday clothes again, and went east to Taft to settle up with Hansi, from whom he had three pounds to get. That same evening he called at the Manse.

"Wal, boss," he said to Mr. Mann, when they were seated in the study, "I guess as haow this blo-bloomin old place is about played out. It aint fit for a decent man to live in naow. The people up here aint got no menners, and no darned sense in their heads. Upon my soul, minister, I feels sorry for the likes of you as has got to stick up here for a constancy, and can't never quit the darned old hole, seein as haow it's your livin so far. Yes, sir, I can't stend it no longer nohaow, an I'm off for the States again, you bet. Wal, I shan't deteen you no longer, but hopes as haow you'll drop us a line naow and then, just to say haow things is goin like. Which I hopes you'll have success with I. BAY., and do out thet great clumsy calf, Bob Ertirson. You take my advice, and give the likes of him and Megni Sharp a wide berth, and, between ourselves, you better keep an eye on thet Perk; he aint no good. Wal, bye-bye, boss; and see and take care of yourself."

He went out, scratching a match on the side of the front door as before. When he had got a short way from the house he turned and put his fingers to his nose.

"You darned fool," he muttered, "I reckon as haow it woon't be long till thet grice Bob Ertirson'll be guidin [treating] you the same as he done me. Jest so. But thet aint none of my business, I guess."

Next morning before daylight he took his trunk, in the locker of which was the tobacco-box with three pounds thirteen shillings in it now, upon his back and made all sail for Lerwick. A fortnight later, Aald Erti said to the neighbours:

"My son Erti was turned fair sick of prostitutin the herring fishin. Well, he perceeds south a couple of weeks ago, and he's now second mate, in a menner of speakin, of a coal brig sailin out of Shiels for the most part."

Mrs. Mann had caught cold that night at the Ha. She did not think about it much at first, and she would scarcely let anything be done for her, for, with her sweet and gentle disposition, she shrank so much from giving others trouble. But at last she had to keep in bed, and the doctor was fetched across the voe. It had ended in becoming inflammation of the lungs, he said, and he had little hope of saving her. She quickly sank.

On the last night, Mann was sitting with her, though he did not know the end was quite so near. She had been very low all day, but late at night she brightened somewhat.

"Are you there, Peter?" she asked faintly, for she did not see him just at first.

"Yes, mother," he said huskily, bending nearer to her. "You are a little better now."

"No, Peter," she said, in a voice that, from her very weakness, sounded sweeter to him now than it had ever done before in all the years that he had hung upon its tones; "I feel that I am sinking fast; but I must speak to you before I go. O, my boy, I wish for your sake I could live a little longer; but I know that it is not to be."

"O, mother, do not say it," he said, his voice thrilling with anguish that he tried in vain to hide from her. "I cannot bear it."

"Hush, Peter," she said softly. "It is His will, and He is with us both. While I am able, I must speak to you. I want you to promise something."

"I will promise anything, mother, anything," he cried; "but O, you must not leave me."

She lay still, looking at him, her great love shining in her eyes.

"You will promise," she said tenderly, "to ask Miss Black to marry you. She loves you, Peter. Last night, when she was sitting with me, she promised me to listen to you. She has been so sweet and good to me in these last days."

"Yes, yes," he answered quickly; "but you must not leave me."

"You have always been loving to me, Peter," she whispered in that sad, sweet voice so soon to murmur itself away into the Great Silence. "In the dark days I had only you, and dear good Naanie. You were my very life, Peter. But there will be no dark days in Heaven where I will meet your father soon, and there will be no anger more, for we shall understand each other in the Light of God. You must lay me by his side in the old churchyard at Lerwick."

She lay quite still again, and her son's sobs were the only sound.

After a long while, she murmured with a light upon her face:

"I see your father, Peter. He is beckoning to me, and there is a Shining One beside him. I come—I come—Lord Jesus."

She passed, and Mann sank on his knees beside the bed in a great agony of prayer.

When Naanie came into the room at four o'clock he told her calmly when it was that the great change had come. But the calm did not endure. Before daylight, he was cursing God. In the blackness into which his soul had sunk he felt that all religion was a lie. He had no belief that her sweet spirit that had passed still lived. It seemed to him that the fair thought of immortality was but an *ignis fatuus* by which Fate led men blindly to the very brink of a great gulf of black despair. But calmer feelings came again, and in the evening Hakki came, and, with tears in his eyes, said, as they held each other by the hand, that he had come to help him all he could, and, while they were together, Mr. Black came in.

Mr. Black, Hakki, and Hansi accompanied him to Lerwick on his melancholy journey.

When the earth fell on the coffin in the old churchyard it seemed that he had braced himself to bear his grief. But he shuddered as he realised that, even in that solemn moment, Inga's image rose before him.

CHAPTER XVI

THE MEETINGS

"Seint er afglapa at snotra."—ICELANDIC PROVERB

WHEN Mann came home again, he could scarcely bear the Manse with that sweet presence gone. For the first few days he wandered constantly from room to room, lingering longest in the room that had been to her gentle soul the very gate of heaven, and looking sadly through its window at the cold, grey sea. It had another window looking north to Taft, but he would not look through it. When he felt that he must look at Taft he went to his own room. Little by little, he began to go there often, to stand looking north at

Taft across the withered heather and the naked fields. At such times he thought of his promise, and muttered to himself that he would keep it sacredly; but that he could not think of it till after a few years had passed. At such times, too, it seemed to him that the church and churchyard lying there between the Manse and Taft rose up as barriers between him and Inga, both guarding silently, the one his work, the other his dead mother's wish.

Black and Perk came to him often; but Perk came seldomer, as he observed that Mann showed little inclination to let friendliness grow into friendship, and they drifted once more from each other. But Mann drew closer now to Black, for he felt that this was moving in the way his promise led, though he was conscious that in feeling so he was but temporising with his difficulty.

His grief had brought him back to something like his former earnestness. Jeems Ertirson came east to see him, and Jeems thought that this great bereavement ought to put a stop to those impending meetings to which he himself was so opposed. It seemed to him, in fact, that it was almost like the hand of God.

"Ye'll hae to let yon meetins be, sir, nu," he said.

"No, Jeems," replied Mann firmly, "I will not let my private grief stand in the way of what I see to be my duty. The meetings will go on." In the past few weeks he had passed through such sickening alternations of hope and despair, of faith and scepticism, shot through with flashes of the passion Inga had excited in him, that he grasped at anything that seemed to offer, even for the moment, a distinct and practicable path. The first time he had gone to Taft he had seen Inga by herself, and she had cried and clung to him in keen, spontaneous sympathy with his great grief. He had, he thought, made up his mind to tell her the whole truth about his promise and his pain; but with a kind of terror he found that he was not able to withstand her nearness to him, for he pressed her to his heart and kissed her passionately. Since then he had gone once a week to Taft. It had occurred to him at times that he would gradually withdraw himself, and so get back, if possible, to the old stage of friendship; but he said to himself that this was mean and cruel. He felt he had now in himself the elements of hell. He knew he could not tell her the plain truth, that in his calmer moments he thought now of this hot love for her as an infatuation, that he really was beginning to try to withdraw himself in spite of his spasmodic feeling of contempt for such a course. But he would throw himself with desperate energy into these meetings. In trying to save others, he might save himself. He doubted now his own effectual calling.

Some time before, he had spoken casually of the meetings to Lamb and Pirie, brethren of the presbytery. Gentle, old Mr. Lamb had warned him earnestly against them, telling him that he would find "Dissent" meant really "Descent" in the long run; but little Mr. Pirie praised Mann's generous view, for he had all along been jealous of Mann's popularity, and wished to see him hurt himself, in which connection Pirie had had two or three long conversations with Aald Erti about certain matters which, with careful treatment, could quite easily become the legs for a good "fama" case to stand upon. Mann thought Pirie always very friendly.

The first snow of the winter was upon the ground the week that Messrs. Howell and Meek arrived, and the fine frosty weather gave the people from a distance a good chance of coming out. Mann could not help a jealous feeling rising in him when he saw the way the church was crowded that first night.

About a dozen westside men had lingered longest at the door. Aald Erti stood expatiating in the midst of them.

"Yes, men," said Erti jerkily, "such meetins is relly very necessitous in a place like this, where we has no life in our sowls, in a menner of speakin, and where there is so much perfession of religion and so little of the real, genuine Gospel, for the most part. Yes, as the Scripter says in one of them parablees, which is sound common sense and no mistake, that a certain man was goin down to Dimaskis, and he fell among tieves, and the thorns sprang up and shoked him, in a menner of speakin.

And it's the very same here now. We hasn't got no Gospel in the pulpit, and what can the place be? The man we have is no use; he can't behave hisself, in a menner of speakin; and there's his preachin—feth, it's the very same as a grice gruntin——"

Mr. Mann opened the door of the vestry and came out, followed by Messrs. Howell and Meek.

"Good evenin, sir," said Aald Erti promptly. "I was just sayin this momment, may *grace be granted,* sir, to us all to profit by the godly preachin you're given us since you comed among us, sir; though them meetins is good also, in a menner of speakin."

"Are you born again, my friend?" asked Howell suddenly, as Mann and Meek passed on into the church.

"Me, sir? Lord bless you, yes, sir,—beg pardon, sir," replied Aald Erti glibly. "Many, many years ago, sir."

Howell said nothing more at the moment, but he put a mark opposite Aald Erti's picture in his memory.

Mann had braced himself for the occasion. He scarcely felt the powerful smell of hair-oil, sweat, and peat-smoke, touched with that of paraffin from one or two imperfectly trimmed lamps, which met them in the face as they came in. He walked in front of Meek and Howell up to the square seat. His voice was passionate as he began with a short prayer, asking God to give each soul the spirit of true earnestness, and take away all false excitement from their minds. Then a psalm was sung, for the people had not got provided yet with Mr. Howell's penny hymn-books.

A prayer by Howell followed, and as Mann listened to this would-be Boanerges, he felt that he had never in his whole life heard such pure impudence used to Almighty God before. He glanced at Meek and once or twice he saw him wince. Then Howell read aloud in a hard, business-like tone the third chapter of John's Gospel, emphasising the eighteenth verse in a way that showed he meant to take it for his text. Next came a prayer by Meek, and, as he listened, Mann felt tears come to his eyes, for the words rose up like the reverent pleading of a child to the Great Father's ear. The whole audience felt its strange, sweet, searching power. It touched them as an echo of the voice of Him who spake in Galilee calling his wandering brothers home, and many wept. Mann thanked God he had brought Meek to the place, for part of his own load seemed lifting now. But Meek sat down, and Howell rose to preach. The spell was broken. In five minutes Howell was painting with wild strokes his picture of the Judgment Day, and in ten more he had got to its sequel, Hell. At this point he became clean frantic, as was to be expected from the nature of his theme, and a long shudder passed among the folk.

Mann saw the colour change on many faces. Inga was with her mother in their pew. He saw her face turn red and white alternately; but he could not bear to look much at her, for he felt that he had done her wrong. She was sitting tortured by the thought of the great change she had seen lately coming over him. She felt that he was drifting from her now, and she was almost desperate.

Howell ceased preaching, and said that he wanted all those who felt themselves lost and wished to be saved to stand up in the course of a prayer, which he would now begin. He started. A westside man stood up on the north side of the church.

"Thank God—there's one," cried Howell, and proceeded.

Another man stood up behind the first.

"There's another—praise the Lord," cried Howell more excitedly.

A young woman stood up in the middle aisle. It was Betty Jeemson.

"Praise God—another; that's three," cried Howell wildly, working up the agony still more in the next section of his prayer.

Mann turned sick. He felt strongly moved to rise and stop the whole proceedings. In a short time Howell had got a dozen up, and then he turned suddenly to Mann and Meek and shouted, as if he were holding on to something that he could not let go for an instant:

"Brethren, go down and speak to them. I will keep on praying."

Mann took the north aisle, Meek the south. Inga was sitting at the outer end of the seat, so that he had to pass quite close to her. She did not look at him. But even his coming near her was too much for her. She fainted. She had been on the point of going into hysterics before. Her father and Mann bent over her at the same moment.

"We must get her to the open air," whispered Mann. Bob and Magni were in their usual seat across the aisle, a little way behind, and Magni felt Bob trembling with excitement. Janny Gair and Ann Ertirson were in the seat in front of them.

Bob's first impulse had been to spring to Inga's side; but he shrank from doing so, with her father and Mann there already. As they passed, carrying Inga out, with Willa following them, a small fur boa which Inga wore and which her father had been trying to take off, fell on the floor; but Willa did not notice it in the dim light. Bob snatched it up. He felt it would be an excuse for going out after her. He was just making up his mind to go, when Janny Gair collapsed right in front of him. She had been meditating fainting for a while, with the view of getting Bob to take her out. He had no option; he was right behind her. He rose, inwardly fuming, and, helped by Magni and Ann, began to assist her out the aisle. When they reached the vestibule, Bob saw Inga sitting limp in a chair which Oli Jarmson had fetched from the vestry. Mann was supporting her head, Willa holding a bottle of smelling-salts to her nose, and Hansi chafing her hands. She was not reviving.

"I think it will be best to take her into the Manse, Mrs. Bolt," said Mann gently, a wave of feeling stirring him. Bob felt as though he could have knocked him down. Hansi and Oli lifted the chair with Inga in it and went out, Mann and Willa following.

Bob and Magni planted Janny in the foot of the gallery stair. Aald Erti had come hurrying out.

"Lowse her stays," said Ann Ertirson, practically, as Bob and Magni lowered Janny into position. Bob shoved his hand into his pocket and pulled out his knife. Next minute he had slit Janny's stay-laces. They parted with a report like that of a pistol.

"Here, look efter your douchter," said Bob gruffly to Aald Erti, and, turning quickly, he hurried out at the church door with Magni after him. As they went, Howell shouted, "There's another!" and women's sobs came from within. Janny opened her eyes, which she had never had entirely closed, and sent a gleam of malice after Bob. She had decided how to put the last peat to her fire of scandal.

"Whar's du goin?" asked Magni nervously, laying his hand on Bob's arm as soon as they had got outside.

"It's aa right. Du needna be frightened," answered Bob, turning towards the Manse. "I'm calm enough."

Inga was lying motionless on the sofa in the dining-room when Bob came softly in, carrying the fur boa in his hand. Willa and Hansi were bending over her, and Mann was standing pale and silent in front of the sofa, and looking down at her. Willa had sent Oli to the kitchen to fetch water. Willa looked up, thinking Bob for Oli; but the others did not move, and Bob stood still. Naanie came hurrying from the kitchen with the water, Oli stumbling behind her. At the first touch of it, Inga stirred, and suddenly opened her eyes. She saw Mann standing right in front of her, in the full light of the table lamp, which he had quickly turned up when they came in. The blood rushed to her cheeks again, and flashes of the hysterical excitement that had mastered her shot from her eyes. All at once she sprang up, crying:

"I am lost—lost! O, Peter, Peter, save me." She flung her arms about Mann's neck, and hung, sobbing, on his breast. He put his arm round her.

Bob set his teeth and clenched his hands, crushing up the fur boa in his right.

Mann's first wild impulse was to throw off all reserve and doubt and coldness, and soothe her as her lover in spite of everything on earth; but, as he raised his head, his eyes fell on his mother's portrait on the wall beside him, and he saw again her pale face on the pillow and heard her sweet voice saying, "You will promise, Peter," as upon that solemn night. He shook with powerful feeling; but a quick revulsion had come over him, and now he all at once thought of the presence of the others.

Inga was conscious, instantly, of the quick change of feeling. She realised that he repulsed her. At such a moment she did not have strength to bear it, and she swooned again. He laid her gently down upon the sofa, and stood motionless in front of it. He feared her reawakening. Her excitement might grow worse. He felt it would be best to leave her to the others and go into the church again. His absence would be looking strange.

"My presence only excites her," he whispered to Willa, "and I must go back to the church now. Naanie will get you a little brandy for her." He passed out with bent head, the skirt of his coat touching Bob as he went. Naanie brought the brandy. A little later, Inga had revived again. She opened her eyes in a dull, slow way. Her excitement seemed in great part to be gone. She knew now where she was; but she saw Mann was no longer there, and a sense of bitter loneliness came to her at the thought that he had so deserted her. She remembered now. Weak as she was, her pride came to her aid. Just as she turned her eyes, she looked right into Bob's. She did not start. It seemed to her, somehow, natural that he should be there. She saw the old, yearning look in his clear, steady eyes. He stood there, big and strong and kind. He was her friend. She suddenly held out her hand to him. With a thrill of joy, Bob stepped to her and took it, tenderly, in his.

"Du'll help me, Bob," she murmured, slowly rising. "I'm better nu. I want ta geng haem."

She took Bob's arm and her mother's and the three went slowly out, followed by Hansi, who was joined outside by Magni. But when they reached the door of Taft her mood had changed, and she gave Bob her hand and said, nervously:

"Tanks ta dee, Bob. Will du geng an tell Hakki ta come ta me?"

CHAPTER XVII

"MAREEL"

"Tant raille-on que plus on ne rit."—VILLON

MAGNI was waiting for Bob at the corner of the house. Bob's blink of hope was once more blackness. They went right up to the Schoolhouse, and Bob entered and told Hakki Inga wanted him. Then Magni got Bob to come home with him to Hooll. They went into the house and sat down by the fire. Magni could think of but one way to comfort him, though he wished from his soul he knew another.

"Bob," he said tenderly, "I loved her long before dee. I've loved her since we were bairns. Du's no alone in sufferin nu." Sudden understanding, pity, admiration, gratitude, surged in Bob's mind; but he said nothing, he only wrung Magni's hand. Later, old Magnus came in from the workshop and went to bed. It was midnight when Bob and Magni parted.

"O, Hakki," cried Inga, clutching his arm as he came in; "he kissed me an said he loved me, an nu he's turned cowld an strange. O, I canna bear it. It's killin me." He stayed a long while with her and got her calmed at last. Then he went out, and quickly south towards the church. The folk had gone home. As Hakki neared the building, two figures appeared in the still lighted doorway. They were Howell and Aald Erti.

"Yes, sir; upon my f-f-fack, sir,—beg pardon, sir,—" cried Aald Erti, shaking Howell vigorously by the hand, "I've never heerd the like of your preachin, sir, afore in my born days. I knows in my blessed experrience that I've got a new haert this night, in a menner of speakin, as I never got afore, sir, and there's just one thing as I'd like to see, sir, for the most part, and that is as how you would go up to-morrow night afore the meetin, like, to old Magnus Sharp's workshop there at Hooll, which is a stronghold of sin and Saatan, sir."

"Is Mr. Mann here?" asked Hakki, coming up.

"No, sir," answered Aald Erti, in a suddenly subdued tone. "It's Mester Meek as is inside. Mester Mann goed away just now." Hakki went on to the Manse. Mann was not there. Hakki said that he would wait.

Mann was down at Da Point, standing there with the cold night air on his hot face and his eyes raised to the sky, now bright with northern lights. He had gone there for a few minutes' peace. Howell's harsh voice and quite coarse personality was jarring on him still; but the scene with Inga was his real pain. He said to himself he could not help it. His passion blew hot and cold; but the thought of marrying her was impossible.

He did not know what to do. Gradually, however, as he stood, the beauty of the scene before him stole into his mind and soothed him in the same way Meek's prayer had done in the church. A deep reverence fell on him. It seemed to him that the Great King was passing by, and he could see the trailing of His purple robes in that fair light that filled the northern sky.

When he reached the Manse, he took Hakki into the study, wondering. Hakki would not sit down. He walked two or three times across the floor, and then stopped suddenly in front of Mann and said, in a cold, hard tone:

"You are killing the girl. Are you a man or a scoundrel? Do you mean to marry her?" The words tore him out of his temporary calm. He felt this to be so impertinent that he grew angry.

"What do you mean?" he asked quickly, looking straight at Hakki.

"That I have let you go too far already," answered he.

"Perhaps it would be necessary for you to show your right to talk as you are doing," said Mann coldly.

"My right would be quite obvious to you if you chanced to have a soul," returned Hakki bitterly.

"You will observe, sir," said Mann haughtily, "that I possess the right to order you out of my house."

"Your house?" sneered Hakki, with a short, hard laugh. "You will observe, sir, that your right to this house is simply that you preach and practice what is called religion, a right you are quite capable of forfeiting." The blood rushed to Mann's face. He felt it hard to keep from striking him. But he controlled himself.

"Yes," continued Hakki fiercely, "there'll be any amount of psalm-singing, and praying, and howling, and any number of these infernal, illegitimacy-producing revival meetings of yours; but for character or manliness, or a common, everyday sense of honour, God help the fool that hopes to find them in the like of you. But of course it does not matter to you. As I said to you long ago, you put your rags in the slot and get a new garment out. You do not care. You do as the Devil bids you, and your Saviour has to pay the bill. As a mere theory, of course, you occasionally mention the possibility of crucifying Him afresh."

The first words stung Mann into rage; the last words cut him to the quick. For a long while he stood looking steadily at Hakki, who saw a strange light come into his eyes, then he said almost gently:

"Will you come upstairs with me?" He took him to the room where Mrs. Mann had died.

Ann was still up when Bob got home. She had gone home from the meeting with Janny who had soon recovered, and a lot of westside lads and lasses, who were keeping close together, for the lasses said that they were frightened, the valley being full of "trows" (trolls), and Janny had whispered something to her and to Osla Moar, something she now ventured to whisper to Bob, thinking it might comfort him in losing Inga, as

Janny had suggested that it would. He turned white with anger when he heard. If Ann had been a man he would have knocked her down. That night he did not go to bed; but wandered about like a restless ghost; though every minute he said to himself it was a lie. He thought of Magni too.

Next afternoon he went to Hooll, looking miserable and haggard from thought and want of sleep. He found Magni in the workshop alone, for old Magnus had gone into the house a while. They sat speaking for a little time, both voices full of suppressed pain and anger; then old Magnus came in from the house again, and they were silent. Aald Erti and Hendri Jeemson came in at old Magnus' back.

"Well, men," said Aald Erti jerkily, "that's a fine evenin, in a menner of speakin, and very shuitable for the time of year." He and Hendri sat down on the broad window-sill, which was their favourite roosting-place when they dropped in along the workshop of an evening. Old Magnus settled himself on his stool, with a very pronounced pucker on his quaint, dried visage.

"Weel, my Erti," he said, lifting up his lapstone, "what news? Dey tell me 'at du's gotten a new haert da last nicht doon by yonder. I warran' it'll be a braa aesy fit for dee yet, for it'll be no graet size, I wid tink. Took du it wi dee, boy; or wis du frichtened to bring it oot for da cowld?" Hendri grinned solemnly. Aald Erti coughed violently and spat. He was disturbed to find that Magnus had the news; but the thought that Howell was now upon his way to Hooll emboldened him. He put on his largest air, and tried to look at Magnus pityingly.

"O, yes, Magnus," he said hurriedly, turning his head a little, as if listening for footsteps, "you may scuff now; but you woon't scuff when you comes to die, for the most part. No, feth, it'll be a different thing then, in a menner of speakin. Yes, I knows in my blessed experrience as how I've got a new haert, which the world cannot give nor cannot take away; for, as the Scripter says, 'Let us never mind the scuffs or the froons of the world, for we all have a cross for to bear,' which is sound common sense, and no mistake. Yes, upun mi sowl, it's the best thing that can happen to a man, in a menner of speakin."

"Dat so," said Hendri, with another solemn grin.

"Du feels aesier nu aboot da Last Day," suggested Magnus, putting on his spectacles.

"Ta be sure," responded Erti promptly.

Quick, firm footsteps passed the window, and Hakki entered, looking troubled, Bob and Magni thought. He had just come from Taft, where Inga lay in bed.

"Fine evening," he said abruptly, and, crossing to where Magni and Bob were sitting, Magni on his own stool and Bob on a box beside him, he took a seat by Bob. The three put their heads together and began a rapid, whispered conversation, the words of which could not he heard by the others, except once, when Hakki hissed out:

"Damnable slander." Then he lit his pipe and began to smoke fiercely, as he usually did when he was very much excited. Magni's dog Starry started barking outside, and Lowra's voice was heard ordering him into the house. A little later, footsteps sounded on the hard snow and a knock came to the workshop door.

"Come in, if yer feet be clean," cried old Magnus cheerily. A hand was heard groping for the latch, then the door opened, and the coarse face of Howell with its hard, black eyes appeared in the lamplight, with the gentle face of Meek behind it.

Aald Erti beamed. Hendri grinned solemnly. The pucker on old Magnus' face grew more pronounced. Hakki, Bob, and Magni looked at the strangers steadily.

"Good evening," said Meek pleasantly, and Hakki and old Magnus echoed. Aald Erti and Hendri got up to let the visitors sit down in the best place.

"I did not see you at our meeting last night, my old friend," said Howell at once, fixing old Magnus with his eye.

"It wid hae been a winder if ye hed," returned Magnus with a chuckle.

"How so?" asked Howell quickly.

"Becaase I wisna dere," replied Magnus thoughtfully. Howell took no notice of this pleasantry.

"Have you found peace?" he asked firmly. "Have you fled from the wrath to come?" His tone indicated very plainly his opinion of old Magnus' state.

"Weel," answered Magnus grimly, "in one way I can't say dat I'm found paece yet."

"In what way?" asked Howell with keen expectancy.

"In the way of rheumatics," returned the old cynic quietly; "an as for fleein frae wrath or onything dat might come efter me, I just couldna do it, for nu I'm not able even to waalk at any graet rate. Na, na; fleein is clean oot o da questin."

Howell knit his brows angrily.

"You are a lost soul," he said. "You are going straight to Hell, straight to a lost and undone Eternity."

"O, brother," said Meek gently, laying his hand on Howell's arm.

"Yes?" said Magnus interrogatively. "An wha tald you dat?"

"Told me that?" repeated Howell sternly. "The Word of God. You are condemned already, condemned as you sit there, because you have not believed on the only begotten Son of God. You have spurned the Saviour."

"I don't think we're mentioned Him da nicht yet," said Magnus quietly.

"You have spurned His servant, sir, and that is enough," said Howell fiercely.

"O, ye're His servant, ar ye?" said Magnus with a smile. "Weel, I widna hae thoucht it, nu. Dis man dat's wi you might raelly be His servant, I tink; bit I'm kind o doobtful aboot you some way or idder."

The words angered Howell still more, for he did not like Meek, who was not his usual colleague, that colleague having turned ill immediately before the present tour. Howell thought Meek much too milk-and-watery for work like this.

"You won't scoff in the flames of Hell," he said hotly. "Praise be to God, I've been washed in the blood of the Lamb, and there is now no condemnation. You can't say that. Ah, no."

"Brother," said Meek again. Old Magnus smiled curiously; but before he could speak, Hakki, who had been getting more and more irritated, spoke.

"Washing in any form is not particularly popular up here," said he with a sarcastic laugh. "You sit quite still now and cool off, while I tell you how I've worked up the washing of regeneration, or rather the regeneration of washing here. It's very interesting. If you won't sit still, I'll feel half inclined to kick you out of this for your impudence to-night."

Howell sat and glared at him for a while, then said in a pugnacious tone:

"I've heard of you."

"Possibly," laughed Hakki, taking his pipe from his mouth. "But hush now." Howell muttered something in his throat.

"When I came here," said Hakki, winking at old Magnus, "I found washing, generally speaking, a lost art. I started teaching it regularly among the other subjects, though there is no grant for it in the code, and almost the entire district was down on me the first day. I presented each youngster with a sponge, each youngster in the place old enough to understand me and to handle it effectively, and insisted on their taking a sponge-bath every Sunday morning to start with, then twice a-week, then three times, and at last every morning. I made it a point of honour with the youngsters, and they have been tractable; but I'm persuading, and coaxing, and bullying, and battle-axing away at some of the adults still. The worst ones are the same blockheads as are now running after you. Now, you get away down to the church to-night and give them a good dressing on the matter, and you'll maybe do a little good for once in your life." Howell rose suddenly from the window-sill.

"You are a child of wrath, even as the other there," he cried. "You mock at the work of the Lord; but you will not mock when you are cast into the lake of fire. Ah, no. But God will laugh at your calamity, and mock when your fear cometh."

"You seem to be a kind of traveller for a big brimstone house and a fire-insurance agent in one, but principally the former," said Hakki with a smile. "Your idea of the Lord's work is amusing. As a matter of fact, about ninety-nine per cent. of what a man like you produces is simply hysterical excitement, superstitious terror, and the crushing of the lasses' hats when they and the lads are going home together. I did not expect you to grasp my doctrine. You are very distinctly more in the fire line than the water, and from certain symptoms I should say my view even as a theory is quite fresh to you."

"The Devil is boiling in the last one of you," roared Howell furiously. "That tongue will roast in

Hell, young man. I have warned you. I have done my duty. I am clear. I shake the dust off my feet against this house."

He stormed out of the shop.

"Yes, sir; upun mi sowl, sir, you done your duty, sir. Wait a momment, sir," said Aald Erti jerkily, hurrying after him, for he feared to stay behind.

There was silence for a while; then Meek said gently:

"If you will pardon me, I should like to speak with you, my friends, about our Greatest Friend." He saw by their faces that they had no thought of jesting with him. Then he spoke of the Master's weary years of loving labour for mankind, and of the love that led Him to lay down His life.

They did not know how soon one of them was to give that final proof of love.

CHAPTER XVIII

TANG

"Willst du immer weiter schweifen?

Sich, das Gute liegt so nah.

Lerne nur das Glűck ergreifen;

Denn das Glűck ist immer da."—GOETHE

WITH that dark thought of Inga, that new danger to her, in his mind, Bob could not rest.

"It is a lie," he muttered to himself again and again. "If I believed it, I would kill him." He haunted Taft, and Magni haunted him.

Howell and Meek had gone, and the dreary quiet of the winter once more lay over Norwik. The approach of Yöl and the New Year made some slight stir of liveliness in a few houses; but Bob was hardly conscious of the days that passed, for Inga still lay in bed tossing with fever, and Bob counted days simply by his trips to Taft each night to speak to Hansi and ask how she was, with as much calmness as he could.

At such times Hansi felt keenly for him. Even Willa had changed in her manner to him, for she was in trouble now herself, and Inga never asked for Mr. Mann. Mann came and asked for Inga every morning, then stood pale and silent in the shop for a few minutes, and so went away again. Folk seldom saw him out.

One night in the last week of the year, Bob had come east to Taft as usual, and had sat a long while downstairs in the parlour, speaking now and then to Willa, when she came down from Inga for a little. At last he went into the shop to Hansi, who was sitting at his desk with a letter he had got that day before him.

"Weel, Bob," he said, rising and coming to the counter, "I'm gled du's come. I see we'll hae ta draa doon da big boat on Seturday, for yon fish must go ta Lerwick ta catch da Monday's steamer. Der nothin comin wir wy till Tuesday."

Bob felt glad that there was to be even this small break in those dark, dreary days.

"It's all 'at ye can do," he said. "I'll get Oli wi me an Magni. We'll hae ta be awa aerly on Monday moarnin."

As he spoke, Janny Gair and Osla Moar came into the shop together, for Osla had come east to spend a night or two at Vatster. Bob's feeling against Janny was so strong that he would not stay in the shop when she was there, and he went out abruptly, saying to Hansi as he went that he would speak to Magni and to Oli.

When he got outside he went right to the south end of the house and stood there in the darkness, under Inga's window, thinking. Then it occurred to him that Janny and Osla would soon be coming past and might observe him, and he went up into the yard, and, leaning against a corn-stack, stood looking up at the lighted skylight of Inga's room, which showed just over the low barn roof. He had made up his mind that next night he would beg Willa to let him come up and see Inga, merely look at her, if only for a single moment, when he heard Janny and Osla coming from the shop again. They paused at the corner of the yard-dyke so that Janny might pin up her skirt more firmly.

"I winder what wy Red-tap is da nicht," Janny mumbled with the pin in her mouth.

"I lippened [expected] dee ta ax Hansi for her," said Osla.

"Me?" returned Janny spitefully. "What am I carin? Shö can be werr afore shö's better, for me; an I doobt sae 'ill be da wy wi her."

"Na, lass," said Osla moderately, "I raelly hopp not, for it wid be a aaful thing."

"Shö's no been da first," said Janny; "an it wid serve her, for da pride o her wis sorely needin a doontak."

"An what's da folk sayin nu?" asked Osla with more interest. "Hae dey ony idder body besides da minister?"

Janny finished with her skirt before replying.

"Dey're sayin a good dael, I'll assure dee," she said; "an it's little winder. Du saa as weel as me what happened yon nicht i da kirk, da very moment 'at da minister cam near her. An du saa da two o dem 'at helpet me, an dan ran oot lack daft things efter her."

"Weel," said Osla; "I toucht shö wid hae nothin ta do wi Bob, an I never heard o ony more."

"Na, der mony a thing du's no heard o, my lamb," said Janny feelingly. "Bob is a poor, saft thing, an aesily led, an far ower good for her; bit, my Faader, lass, der been a wark wi lads 'at's no been little. My bridder Erti tald me 'at wan nicht he hed his airm aboot her neck himsell an shö wantet him ta tak her oot ta da States wi him. He wisna wantin her or he could hae mairried her whin he laeket. Bit he noticed whin he wis oot aboot da nichts, an he saa everything 'at wis goin on, an I'll assure dee, der dem here 'at's a dael deeper dan ye wid think. Frae what he tald me an what he saa himsell, I firmly believe 'at if der onything wrong an it's no da minister, dan it's——"

Bob stood listening breathlessly to catch her words; but she whispered the name so low in Osla's ear that he lost it altogether, and, in his excitement, he could hardly keep from uttering an exclamation.

"Na, lass," said Osla sceptically, "dat's oonpossible."

"Yes, Magni Sharp," repeated Janny in a louder whisper. "Hooll is very haandy wi Taft, du kens."

This time Bob did not lose it. He leaned back heavily against the corn-stack as if he had been struck. The jealousy and suspicion that had tortured him had never before taken this direction, had never, he thought, had occasion to do so, for Magni was his friend, and he believed in him. But now the thought of Magni's brief confession, made that night when Inga fainted in the church, rushed on his mind with quite new force, and he remembered now that Magni had not said so much as he had felt sure that he would next evening in the workshop, when he had told him of what Ann had whispered to him on the previous night. He pushed low thoughts of Magni from him, but they came again. He was so confused by his conflicting feelings that he did not know exactly when Janny and Osla went away.

After a while he came out from the yard, and turned up the hill. He thought he would go to the Schoolhouse for a little and see Hakki, who would, he knew, be shortly coming down to Taft. He felt he could not go to Hooll just then, as he had meant to do when he came out from Taft. But, all at once, the whole thing seemed to him utterly preposterous, and he wondered how he could have harboured such a thought of Magni even for an instant. He faced round and went up towards Hooll. But he had gone only a few steps when his own morbid thoughts stopped him again. He had nursed too long the habit of suspicion, and, like a snake, it turned on him now, deadly and blind, unable to distinguish friend from foe. For a while he stood there, irresolute; then he turned and started doggedly west for Sætter, wondering every other minute at himself for being driven now like a dismasted craft before a storm of dark suspicion that had been raised by nothing but a poisoned sentence from the black tongue of a slanderer like Janny Gair. He did not know that Magni came behind him till he had got past the Schoolhouse.

Magni could not understand why Bob did not come up to Hooll. Once or twice as he went after Bob he thought to call to him; but he did not, for he felt certain Bob was troubled about something, and he would not force himself upon him when it seemed as if he wished to he alone. As soon as he was quite sure that Bob did not mean to come to Hooll, he turned and walked off quickly down the hill to Taft. There Hansi told him and Oli, who had chanced to come into the shop, about the trip that must be made to Lerwick.

Next afternoon Bob came to Hooll to speak about the boat, and he told Magni that he thought it would be best to draw her down at high tide before daylight on Friday morning. He was really anxious for some distraction from his own tormenting thoughts. He was very silent and preoccupied. Magni felt that some strange coldness, he could not explain, had suddenly come between them; but, in his strong way, he made up his mind to bear this too, believing all would soon come right again. Once or twice Bob cheered up a good deal, and Magni thought to rally him as usual about running off last night; but something held him silent.

At high tide before daylight on Friday morning the "Inga" was drawn down. As soon as Bob was busy, his manner towards Magni seemed to get back to its old cordiality. Magni responded generously, and in the shop on Saturday night they were to all appearance as before.

While they were standing there, Willa came in from the house and said to Bob:

"Inga is a lot better da nicht. Da doctor says 'at shö can rise nu in a day or twa, for da fivver is been aff o her a braa while nu."

Then Willa suddenly bent close to Bob and whispered; but Magni could not help hearing what she said:

"Shö says 'at shö wid laek to see dee, whin du comes back frae Lerwick."

Bob was looking right at Magni over Willa's head. He saw a strange light shining in his eyes, and the hot blood mounting to his face. His black thought came to him again; but, afterwards, he knew that this was friendship fighting its last fight with love and conquering. His own feelings swelled now to a tumult in him. Hope and suspicion tortured him. He did not know what he would hear from Inga when they met.

As he and Magni went home together, he scarcely spoke. Next day's inaction left him free to brood once more.

A little after midnight on the Sunday night, the "Inga" started on her voyage to Lerwick. The wind was from north-east. Again and again upon the passage, Bob felt moved to bridge the chasm between him and Magni; but a dumb devil had now entered into him, and the words stuck in his throat. Several times Magni spoke to him in his old way, but he could not bring himself to answer freely.

On their way home again he had grown worse. He sat steering, with Magni close beside him. Oli was forward at the mast. Magni felt sure Bob was thinking about Inga. Once he tried to comfort him, for he believed her message could have but one meaning, which was hope, nay, practically certainty.

"It'll aa be richt son nu, boy," he said cheerily. Bob only gave a grunt in answer.

When they reached the entrance of the voe, it was nearly nine o'clock. The wind had risen. The night was very dark; but they could see the lights of home, and each of them on board knew every stone along the shore. Magni saw the bright lamp shining out from Hooll, like a light up in the sky.

Up at Hooll the wind was blustering about the house. Old Magnus opened the door and looked out, then he went back to the fireside and said to Lowra:

"Aye, lass; he's a tirss o wind. Da Enga 'ill be comin flyin up da voe wi her cotts ower her head da nicht."

"O, faeder," said Lowra with a smile, which was her last for many days. The old man never made a joke again.

Hakki had been at Hooll a while, and had gone down to Taft.

The "Inga" was now coming dead before the wind, and Magni knew well from the way she yawed that Bob was steering much more carelessly than usual. He spoke to him, but Bob did not answer.

Suddenly he dimly saw the dark mass of the mainsail swoop towards him. The boat had jibed. Instinctively he ducked, and called to Bob. Bob ducked too late. The boom struck him on the head and shoulder and sent him headlong overboard. Magni saw him go.

"My God!" he cried, and instantly sprang after him.

Oli ran aft at that cry. He seized an oar and flung it out into the darkness to them; then, jamming the helm down with his foot, he hauled in the mainsheet and brought the "Inga" to the wind as fast as he was able.

Magni, blinded and choked by the chopping sea, the icy spray lashing in his face, had got hold of Bob, and was supporting him with difficulty, for the blow had made him senseless. He had not seen the oar that Oli threw. He and Oli shouted to each other. At last Oli, now half frantic with excitement, got the boat close to the shouts, which had grown weaker every time. Then all at once he heard a cry out of the darkness right alongside. He flung a rope and leaned out over the boat's rail. A foam-topped wave bore a dark mass towards him. He heard Magni gasp:

"O, Christ! Be quick!" He made a clutch and got Bob by the jersey, dragged him on deck, and turned wildly to help Magni. Magni was gone.

Hakki and Hansi had heard the shouts and had run down to Da Point. When Oli, after fruitless trying, at last ran the boat into the cove and beached her in the shelter of the rocks, he whispered hoarsely that both men were dead.

Bob was taken up to Taft and laid in bed.

Inga, in spite of all that Willa and the rest could say, came down and sat by him to watch for his awakening. Far out in the night he opened his blue eyes and saw her there.

"I never believed it, Inga," he murmured after he had lain a while struggling to remember. She knew what he meant, for Betty had told Willa what the folk were whispering; but she forgave him.

With Magni's death, a great gloom fell on Norwik. On the third day, at high tide, before daylight, his body came into the cove, and when the gray winter dawn came up his dog Starry stood there howling over it. Bob and Hakki found their dead friend there, with the fearless look frozen on his face and the brown fronds of the seaweed waving round him, and they knelt down beside him on the cold, wet sand and cried like children. He was laid in the churchyard by the shore, and in the spring old Magnus was laid there beside him.

On the last Sunday of the following year, the Rev. Peter Mann said from the pulpit:

"There is a purpose of marriage between Robert Ertirson and Inga Bolt, both residing in this parish."

And out on the white sand of the little cove among the black rocks of Da Point, the restless waves washed to and fro the brown fronds of the "TANG."

SUBSCRIBERS

This inaugural book of the series could not have been published without the invaluable assistance of those who subscribed via a crowdfunding platform. The series editor and publisher would like to acknowledge their help with their heartfelt thanks, and, in time-honoured tradition, with public salutation in the following list:

Hazel Anderson; Amy Arthur; Timothy Baker; Joan Blanch; Margaret Blance; Helen Bowell; Eileen Brooke-Freeman; Fiona-Jane Brown; John Cairns; Siún Carden; Wilma Cluness; Eleanor Coghill; Laura Dalgarno-Platt; Jenny Davidson; Christine de Luca; Karen Duncan; Catherine Emslie; Erin Farley; Allen Fraser; Liz Garrick; Arnina Goodlad; Lynn Goodlad; Ruth Graham; Gundel Grolimund; Janice Halcrow; Alistair Hamilton; Neil Hay; Brian Holton; Kathy Hubbard; Christine Hunter; John Hunter; Kareen Hunter; Nancy Hunter; Joanne Jamieson; Karen Jamieson; Catherine Jeromson; Angus Johnson; Ingri Johnson; June Johnson; Karl Johnson; Gordon Johnston; Stephen Johnston; Magnus Laurenson; Ian Loudon; Charlotta Malm; Simon

Manfield; Paul Manson; Stanley Manson; Graham March; Fiona MacInnes; Derrick McClure; Catherine McDonald; Morag McGill; Duncan McLean; Joan Michael; Alison Miller; Tim Morrison; Jim & Rosabel Nicolson; Elizabeth Park; Pam Perkins; Catherine Post; Sheenagh Pugh; Kathryn Ramsden; Vaila Randle; Neil Ritch; Margaret Roberts; James Robertson; Sheila Robertson; Carla Sassi; Magnus Shearer; Jane Shouesmith-Black; Isabel Sinclair; Marina Sinclair; Beryl Smith; Brian Smith; Dale Smith; Ingrid Smith; Janet Smith; Jen Stout; Linda Sutherland; Christine Tait; Marsali Taylor; Antonia Thomas; Ann & Ian Thomson; Margaret Tong; Jean Urquhart; Judith-Ann Wardlaw; Joyce Wark; Kenny Watt; Martin Watt; Elizabeth Williamson; Magnus Williamson.

Robert Alan Jamieson & Mike Walmer,

January 2021

Lightning Source UK Ltd.
Milton Keynes UK
UKHW041700241022
411005UK00006B/1275

9 780648 920427